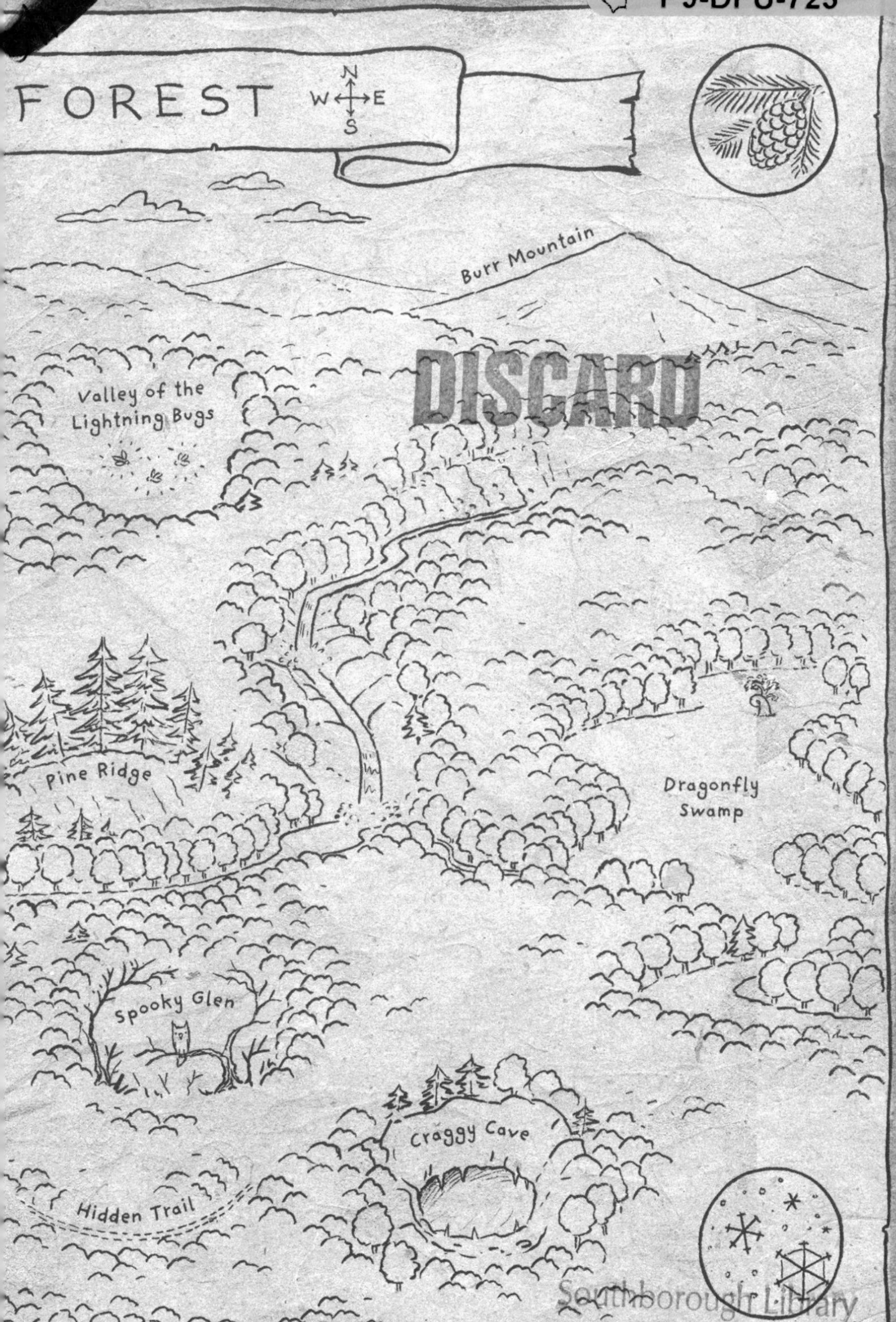
FOREST
N
W
E
S
Burr Mountain
Valley of the Lightning Bugs
Pine Ridge
Dragonfly Swamp
Spooky Glen
Craggy Cave
Hidden Trail

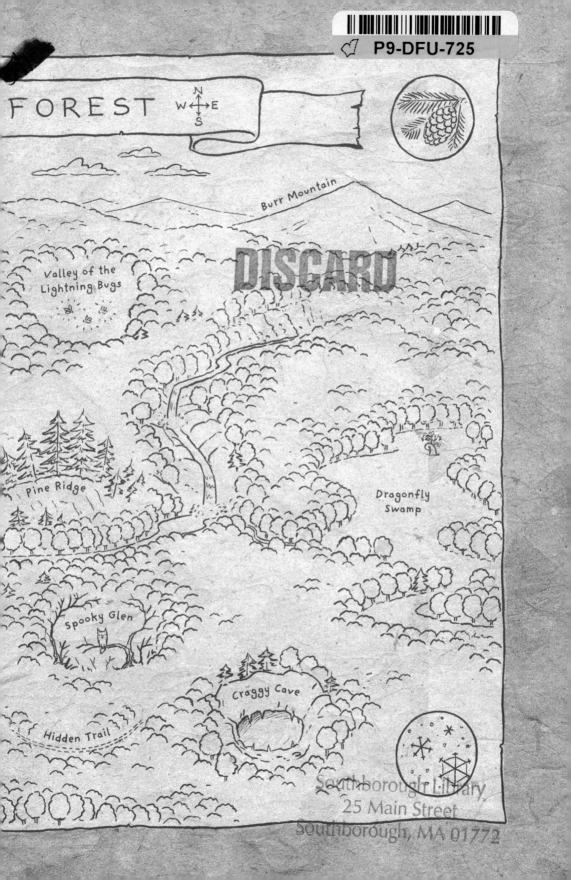

STICKY 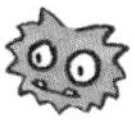

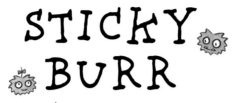

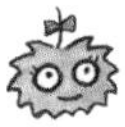 BURR

Adventures in
Burrwood Forest

BURR: (n) the rough, prickly seedcase of certain plants

STICKY: (adj) tending to cling to things; difficult to deal with

PROLOGUE

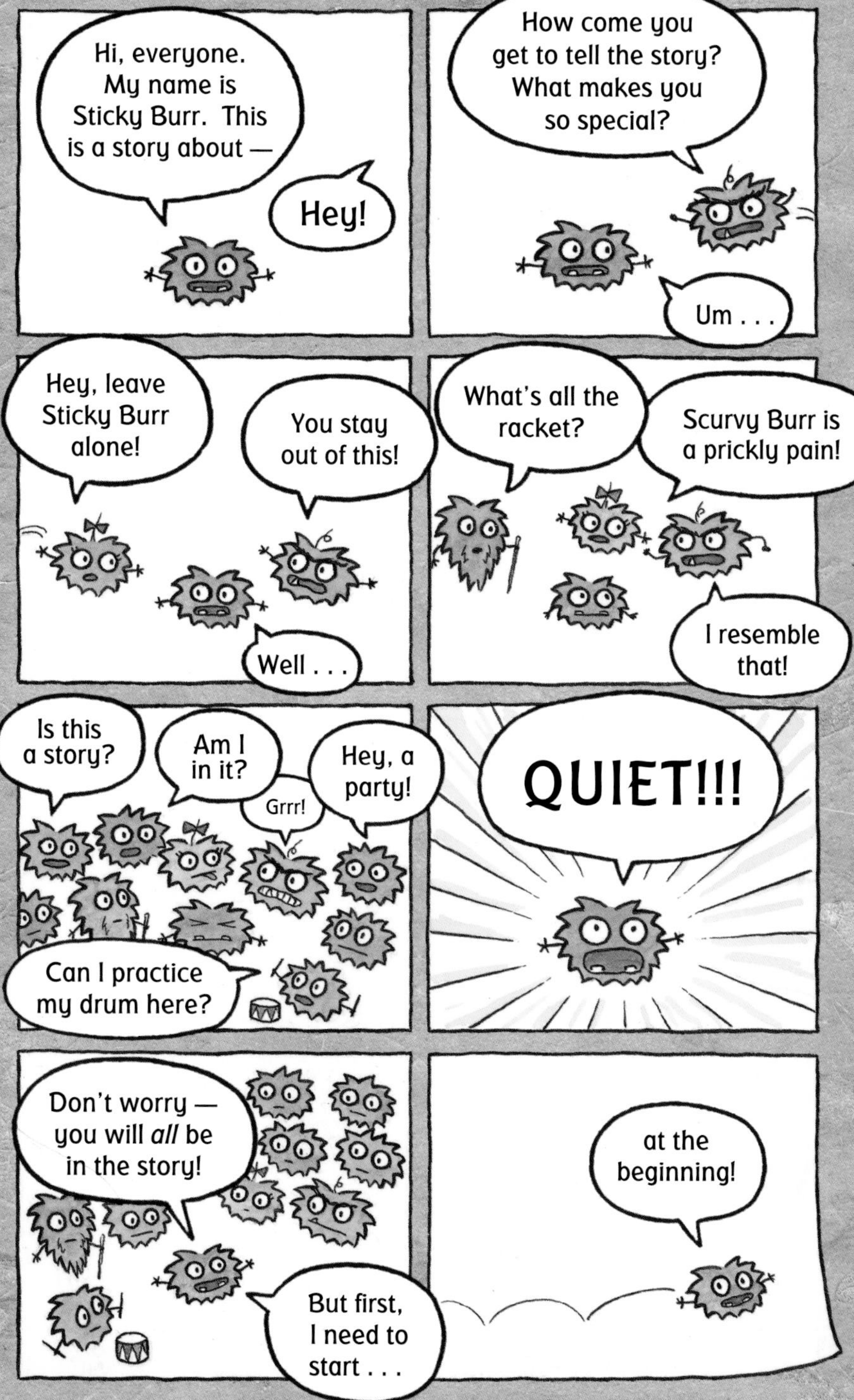
Hi, everyone. My name is Sticky Burr. This is a story about —
Hey!
How come you get to tell the story? What makes you so special?
Um . . .
Hey, leave Sticky Burr alone!
You stay out of this!
Well . . .
What's all the racket?
Scurvy Burr is a prickly pain!
I resemble that!
Is this a story?
Am I in it?
Grrr!
Hey, a party!
Can I practice my drum here?
QUIET!!!
Don't worry — you will *all* be in the story!
But first, I need to start . . .
at the beginning!

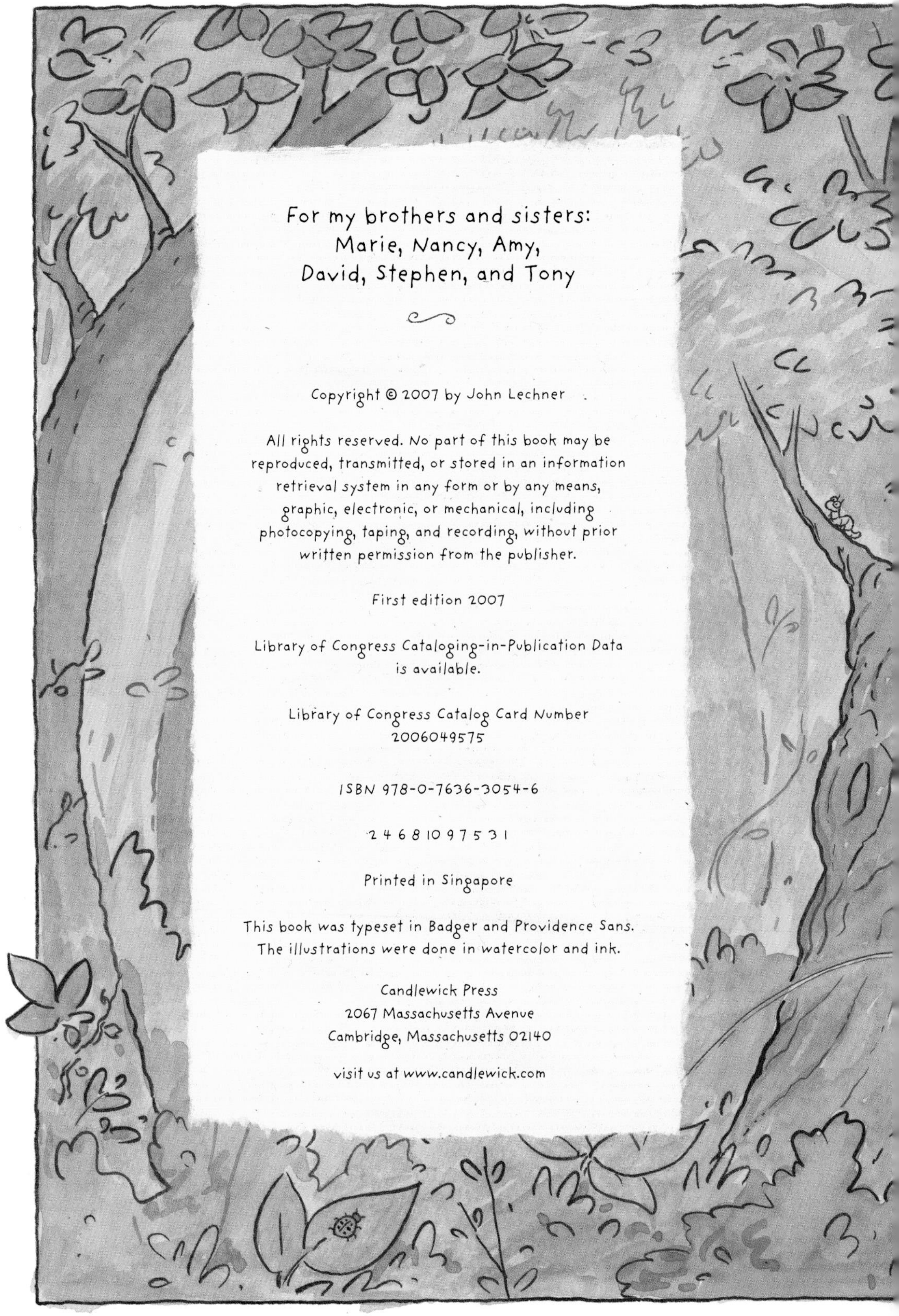

For my brothers and sisters:
Marie, Nancy, Amy,
David, Stephen, and Tony

First edition 2007

Library of Congress Cataloging-in-Publication Data
is available.

Library of Congress Catalog Card Number
2006049575

ISBN 978-0-7636-3054-6

2 4 6 8 10 9 7 5 3 1

Printed in Singapore

This book was typeset in Badger and Providence Sans.
The illustrations were done in watercolor and ink.

Candlewick Press
2067 Massachusetts Avenue
Cambridge, Massachusetts 02140

visit us at www.candlewick.com

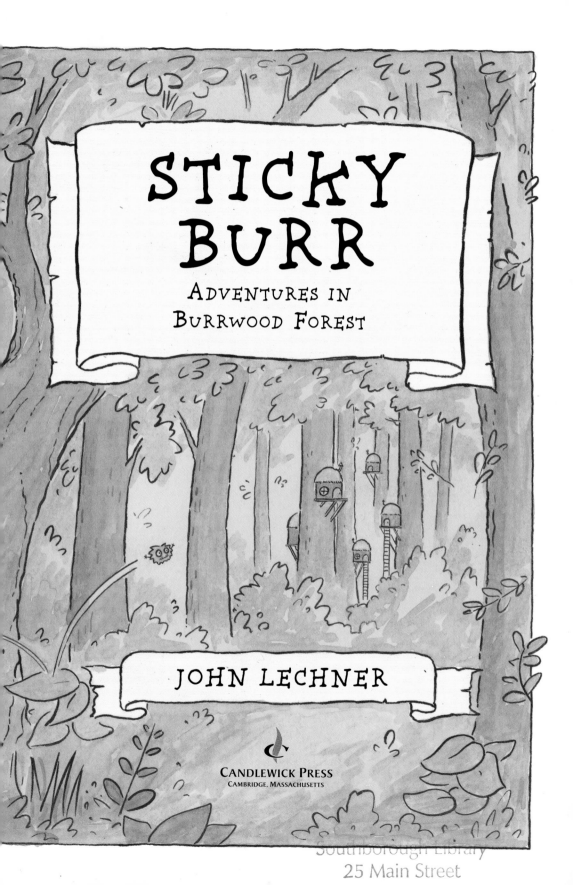

STICKY BURR

BURR

ADVENTURES IN BURRWOOD FOREST

JOHN LECHNER

CANDLEWICK PRESS
CAMBRIDGE, MASSACHUSETTS

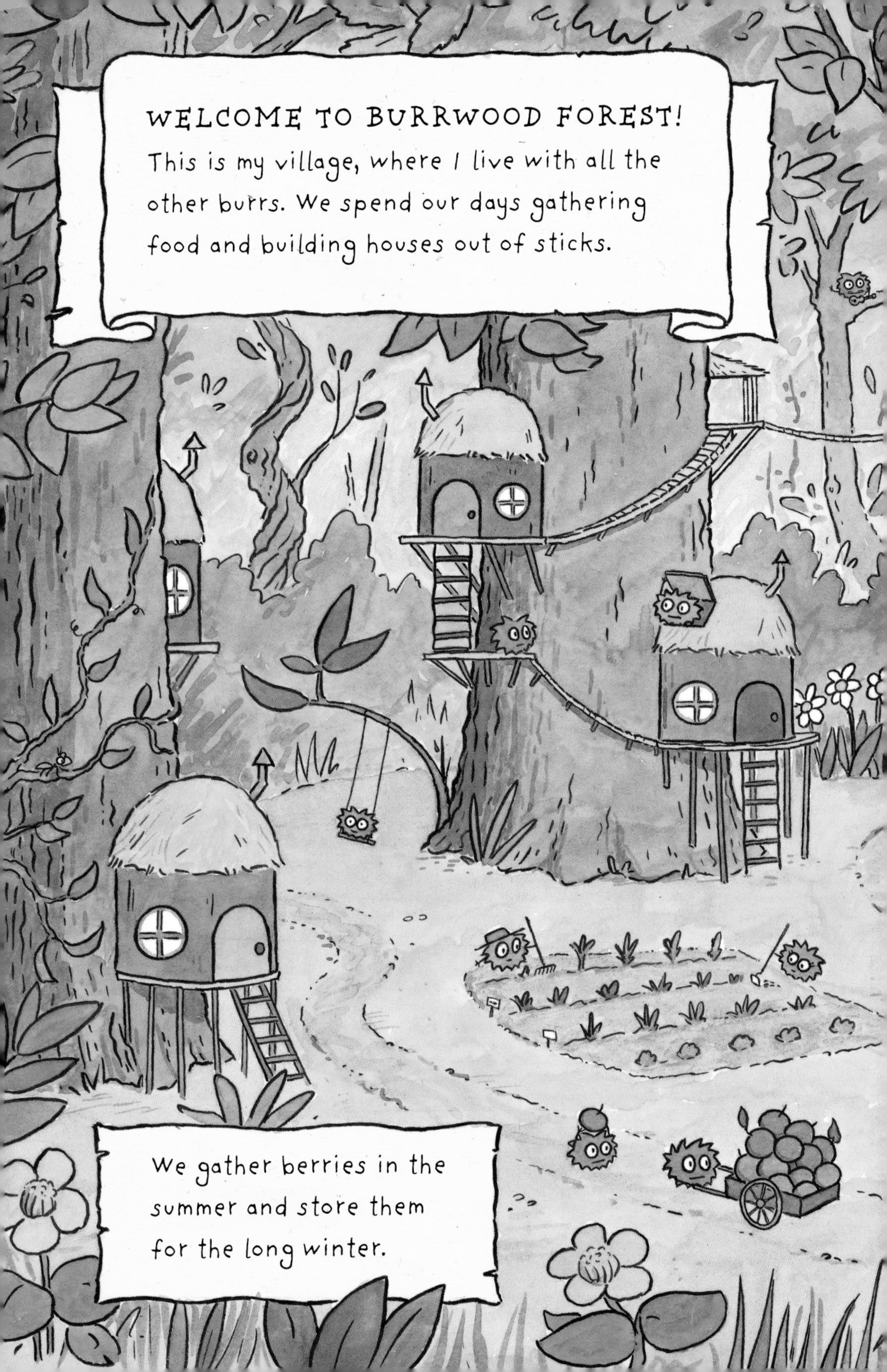
WELCOME TO BURRWOOD FOREST!
This is my village, where I live with all the other burrs. We spend our days gathering food and building houses out of sticks.
We gather berries in the summer and store them for the long winter.

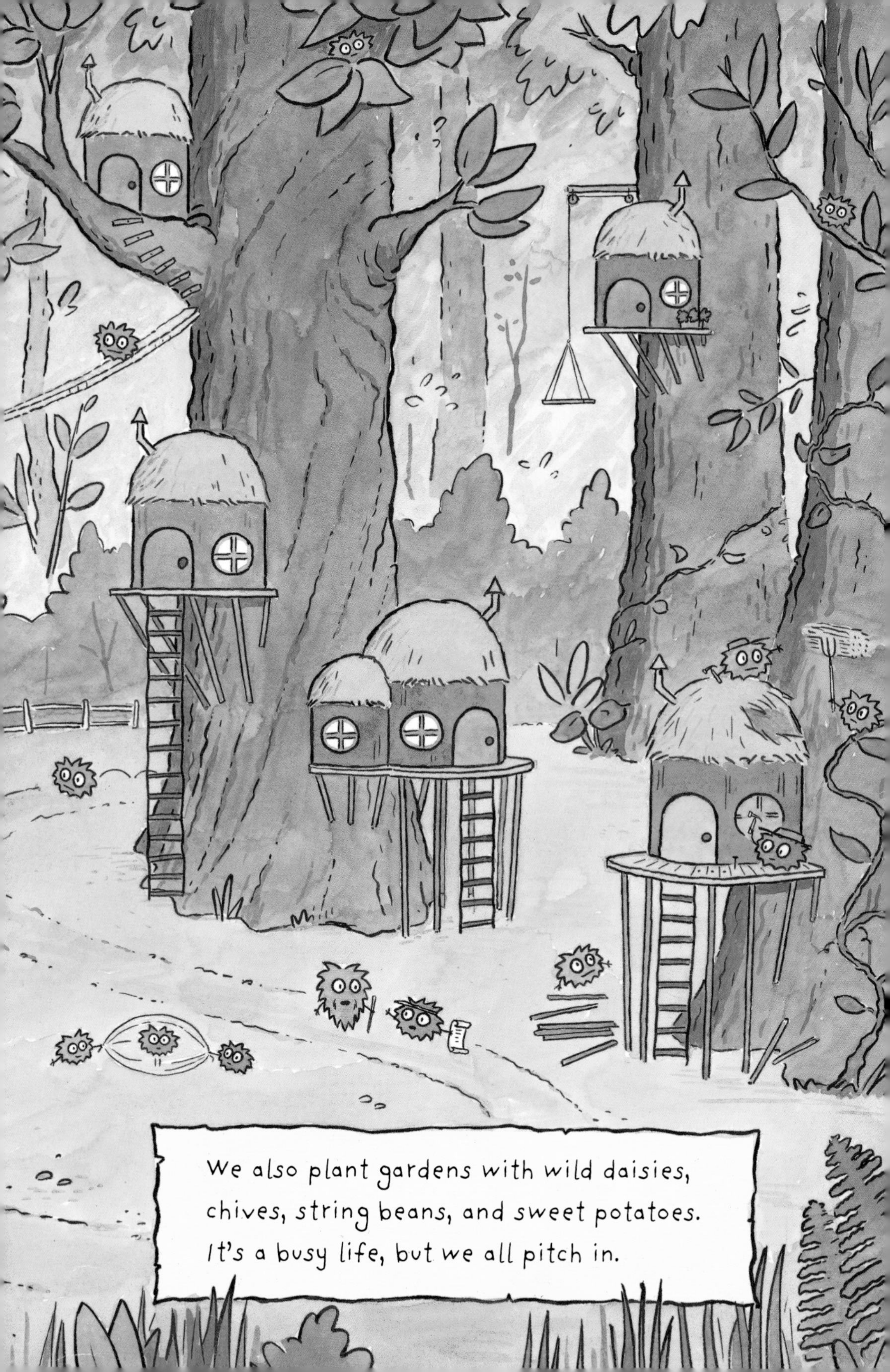
We also plant gardens with wild daisies,
chives, string beans, and sweet potatoes.
It's a busy life, but we all pitch in.

~ ALL ABOUT BURRS ~

Me

My Journal

Let me tell you a little more about burrs. We are very small and covered with tiny hooks, so we stick to things. Sometimes this can be very inconvenient!

Me
getting
stuck

We tend to argue
a lot, even when
there is nothing to
argue about.

No, we
don't!

Yes,
we do!

I'm hungry!

Our houses are built high off the ground, on stilts. Here is a picture of my house—I built a special elevator to get up and down fast.

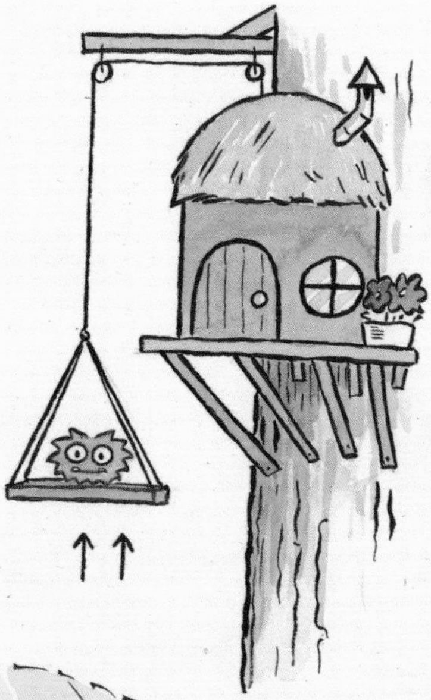

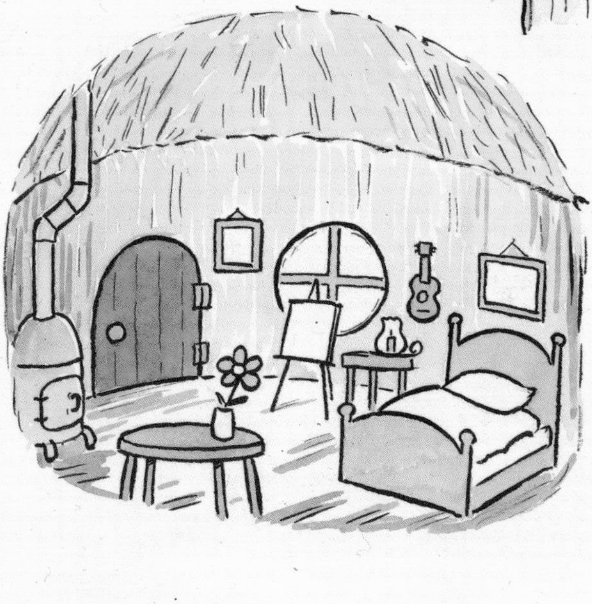

And here is the inside—nice and cozy!

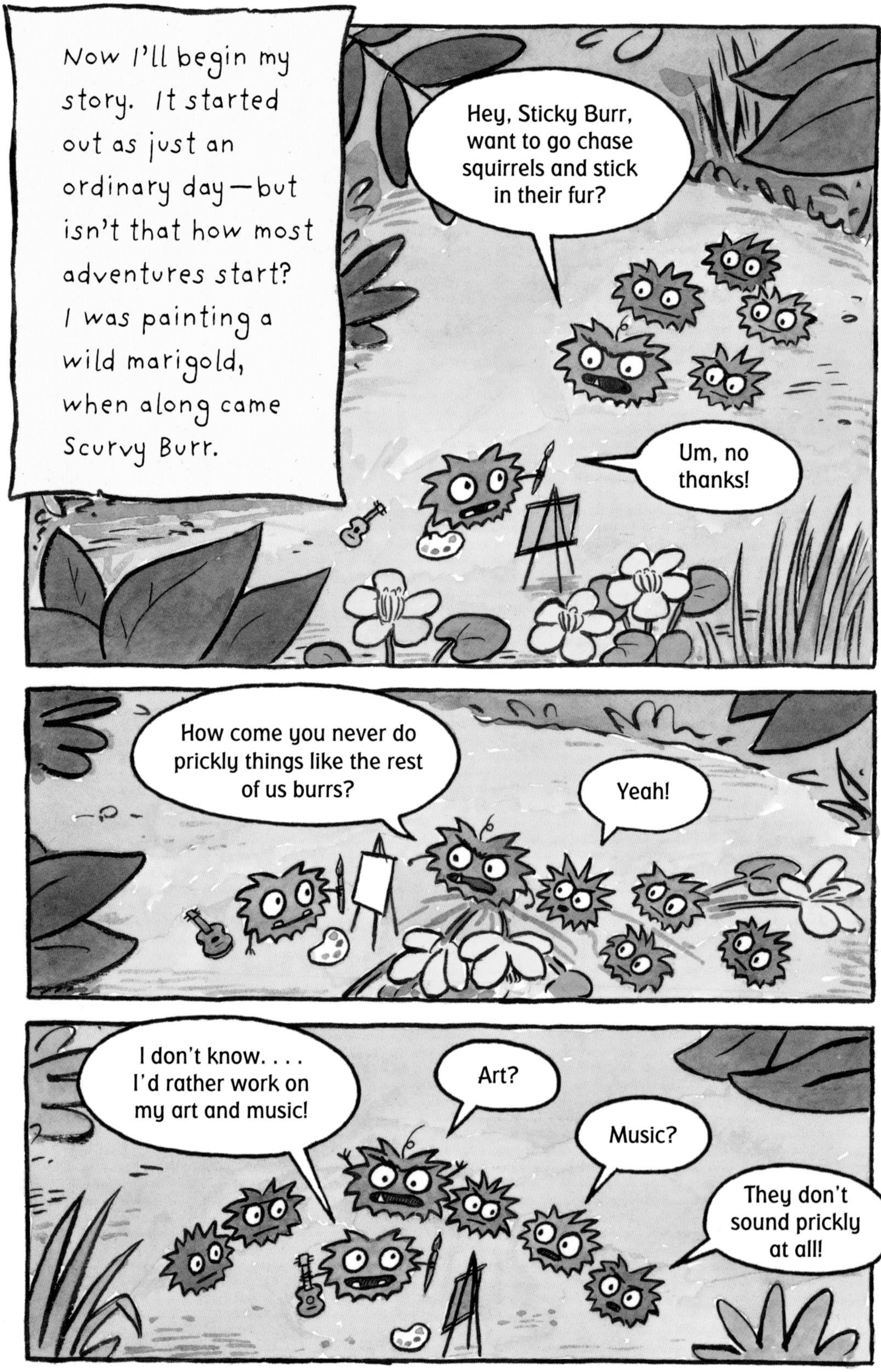
Now I'll begin my story. It started out as just an ordinary day—but isn't that how most adventures start? I was painting a wild marigold, when along came Scurvy Burr.
Hey, Sticky Burr, want to go chase squirrels and stick in their fur?
Um, no thanks!
How come you never do prickly things like the rest of us burrs?
Yeah!
I don't know. . . . I'd rather work on my art and music!
Art?
Music?
They don't sound prickly at all!

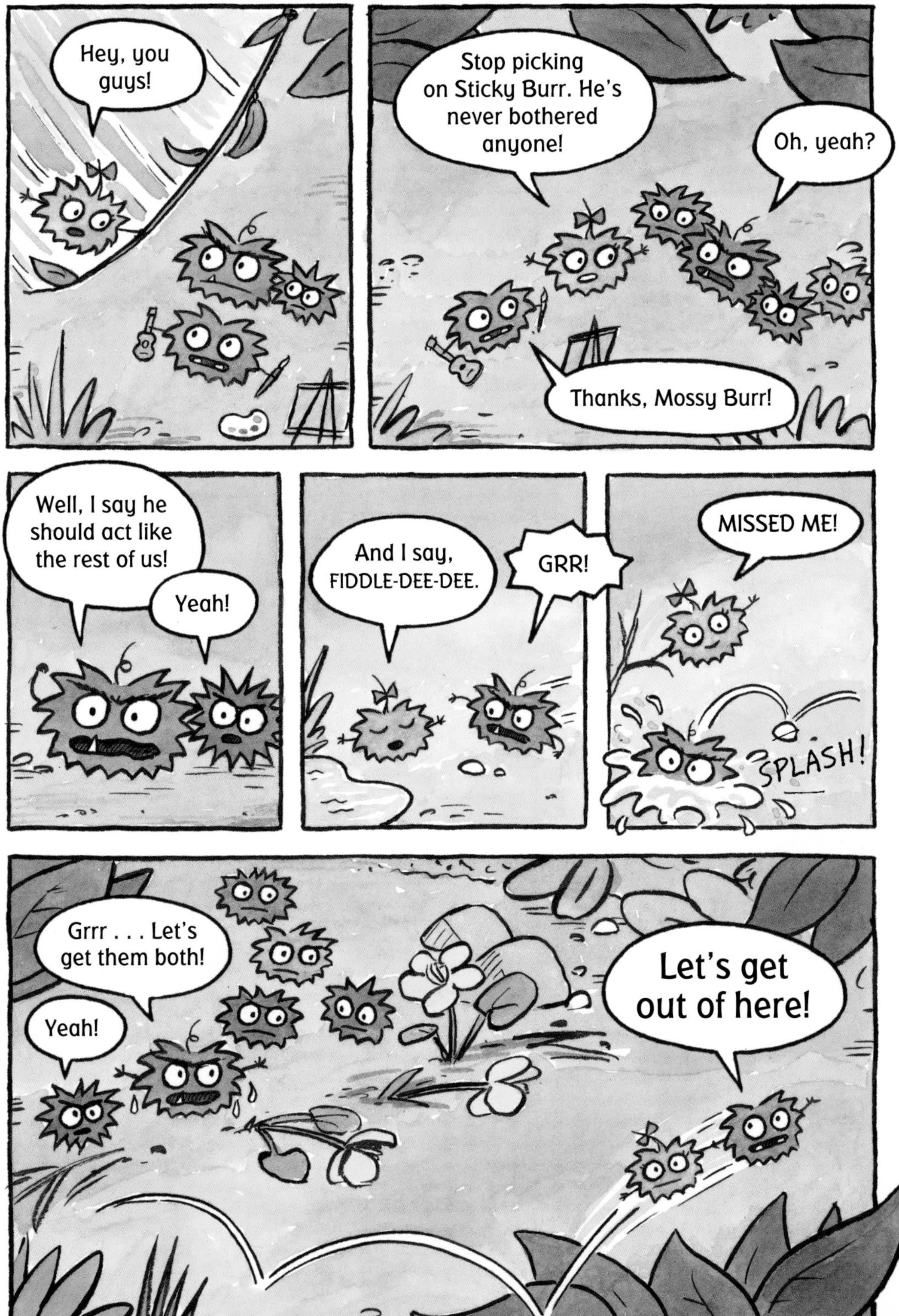
Hey, you guys!
Stop picking on Sticky Burr. He's never bothered anyone!
Oh, yeah?
Thanks, Mossy Burr!
Well, I say he should act like the rest of us!
Yeah!
And I say, FIDDLE-DEE-DEE.
GRR!
MISSED ME!
SPLASH!
Grrr . . . Let's get them both!
Yeah!
Let's get out of here!

SCURVY BURR

Scurvy Burr is always up to no good. You might say he's a bad seed.

He is only having fun when he is making someone else NOT have fun.

He chases crickets.

He tramples flowers.

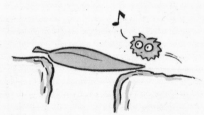

He sets traps.

He even takes candy from baby burrs!

His sidekick is called Spiny Burr—he's nasty, too!

~ YEAH!

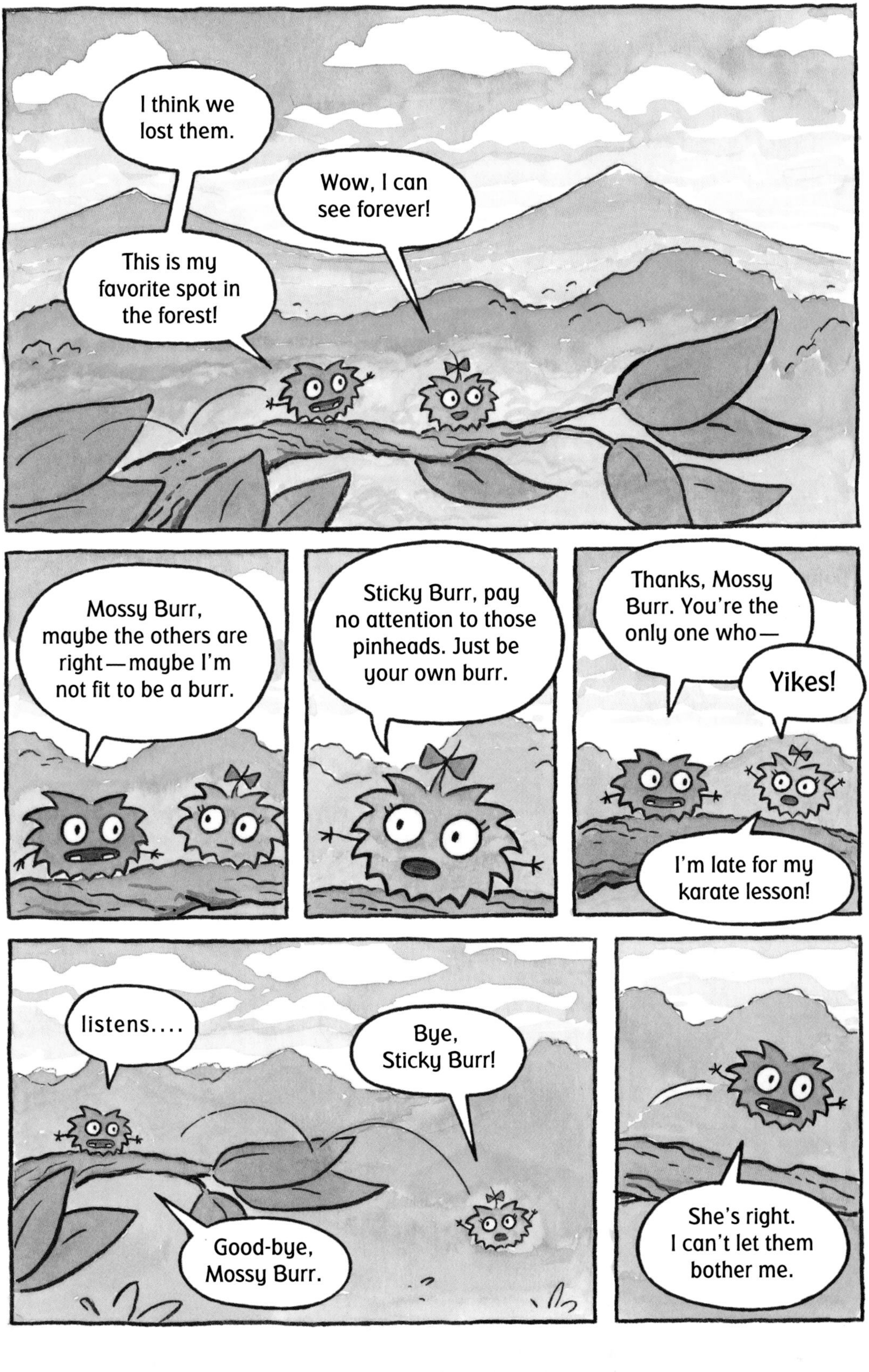
I think we lost them.
This is my favorite spot in the forest!
Wow, I can see forever!
Mossy Burr, maybe the others are right—maybe I'm not fit to be a burr.
Sticky Burr, pay no attention to those pinheads. Just be your own burr.
Thanks, Mossy Burr. You're the only one who—
Yikes!
I'm late for my karate lesson!
listens....
Bye, Sticky Burr!
Good-bye, Mossy Burr.
She's right. I can't let them bother me.

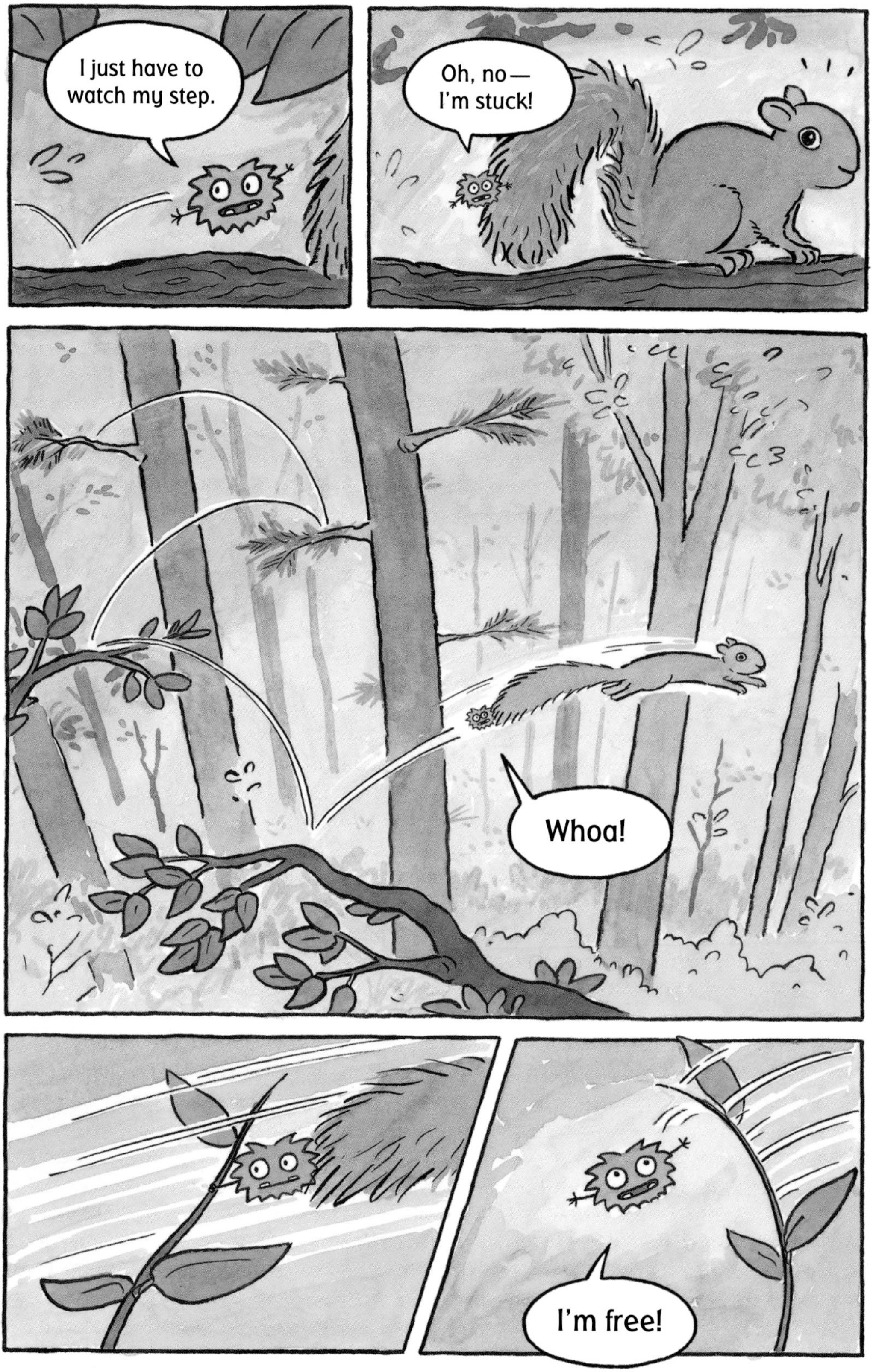
I just have to watch my step.
Oh, no— I'm stuck!
Whoa!
I'm free!

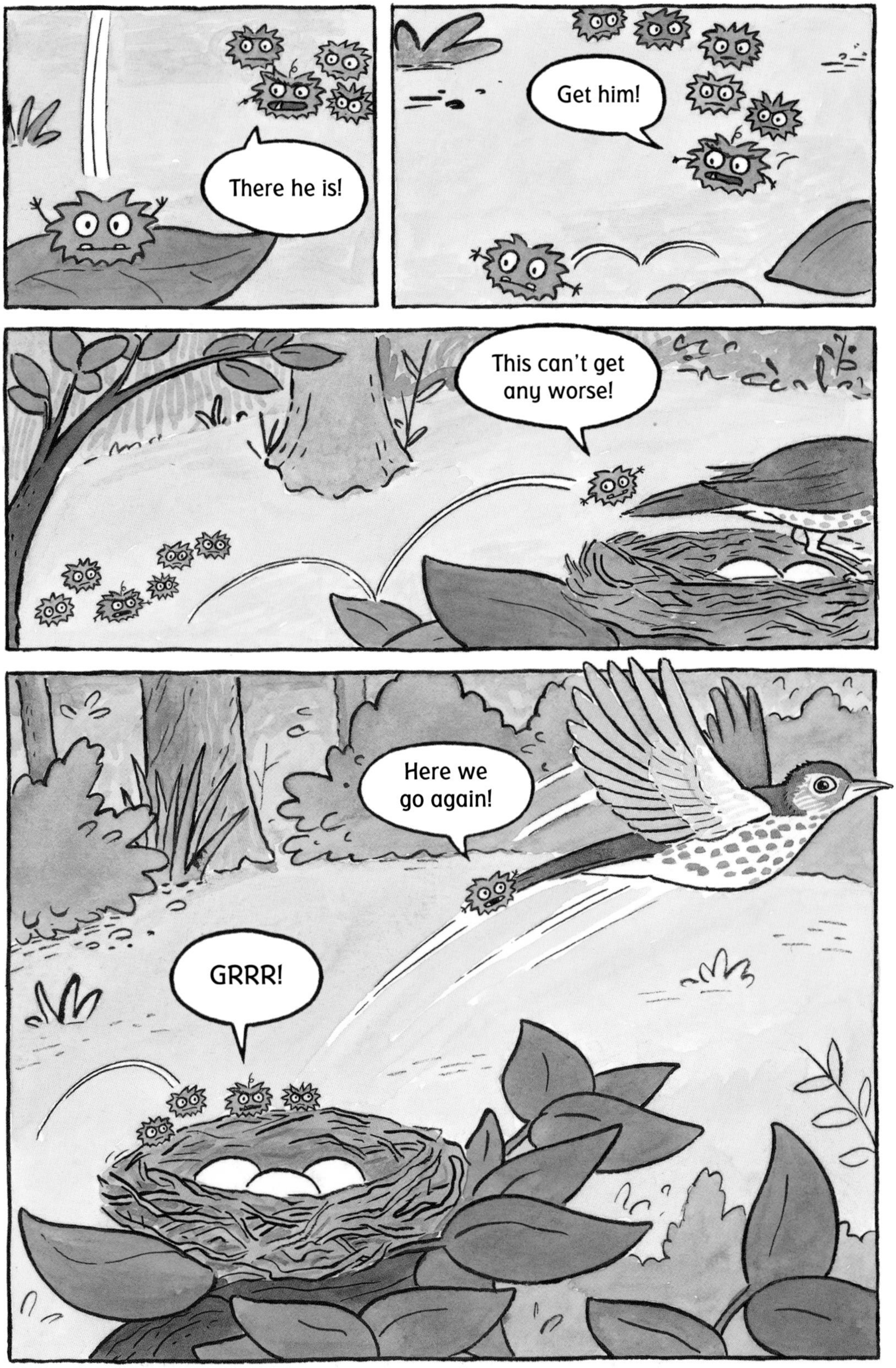
There he is!
Get him!
This can't get any worse!
Here we go again!
GRRR!

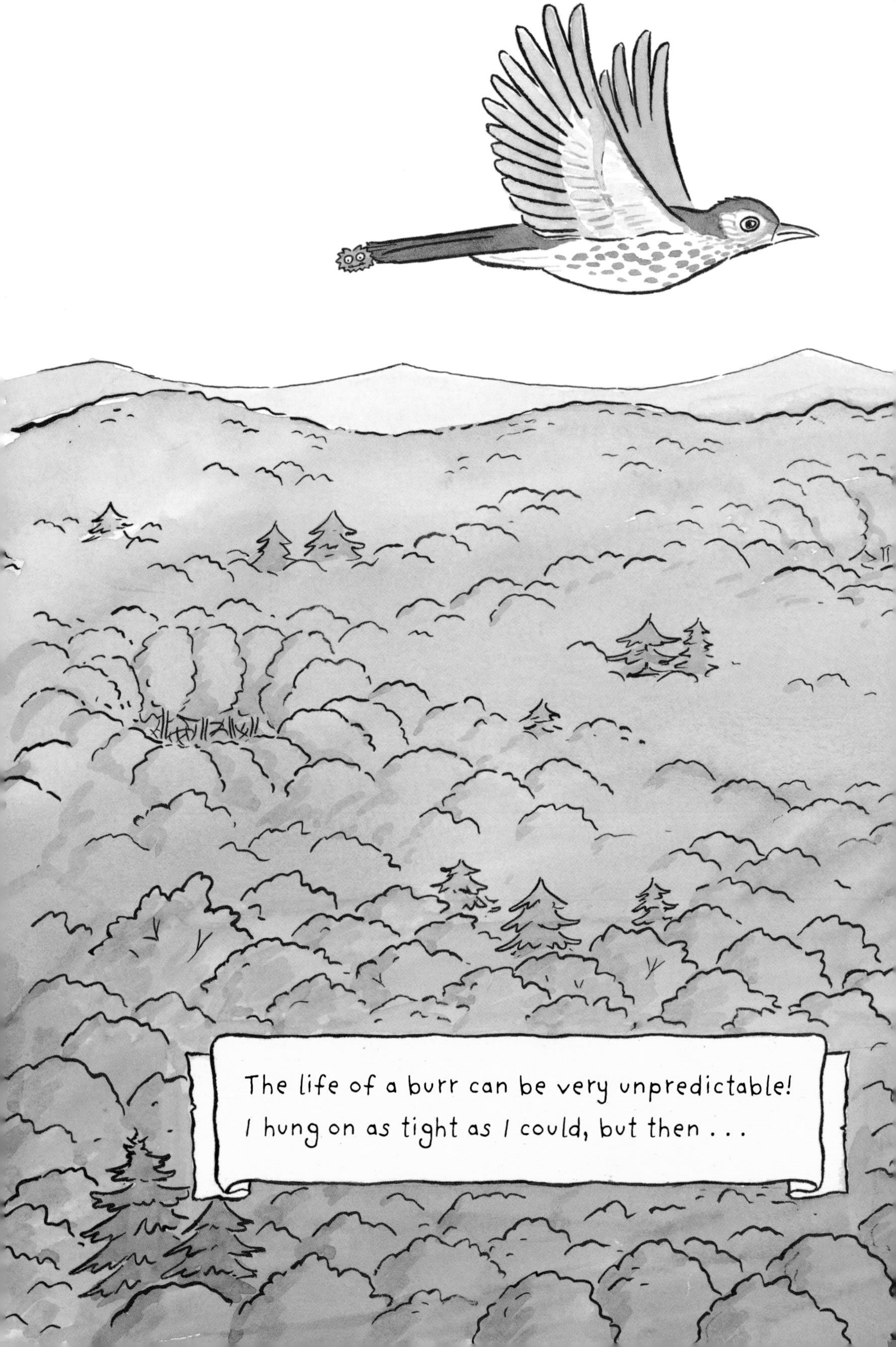
The life of a burr can be very unpredictable!
I hung on as tight as I could, but then . . .

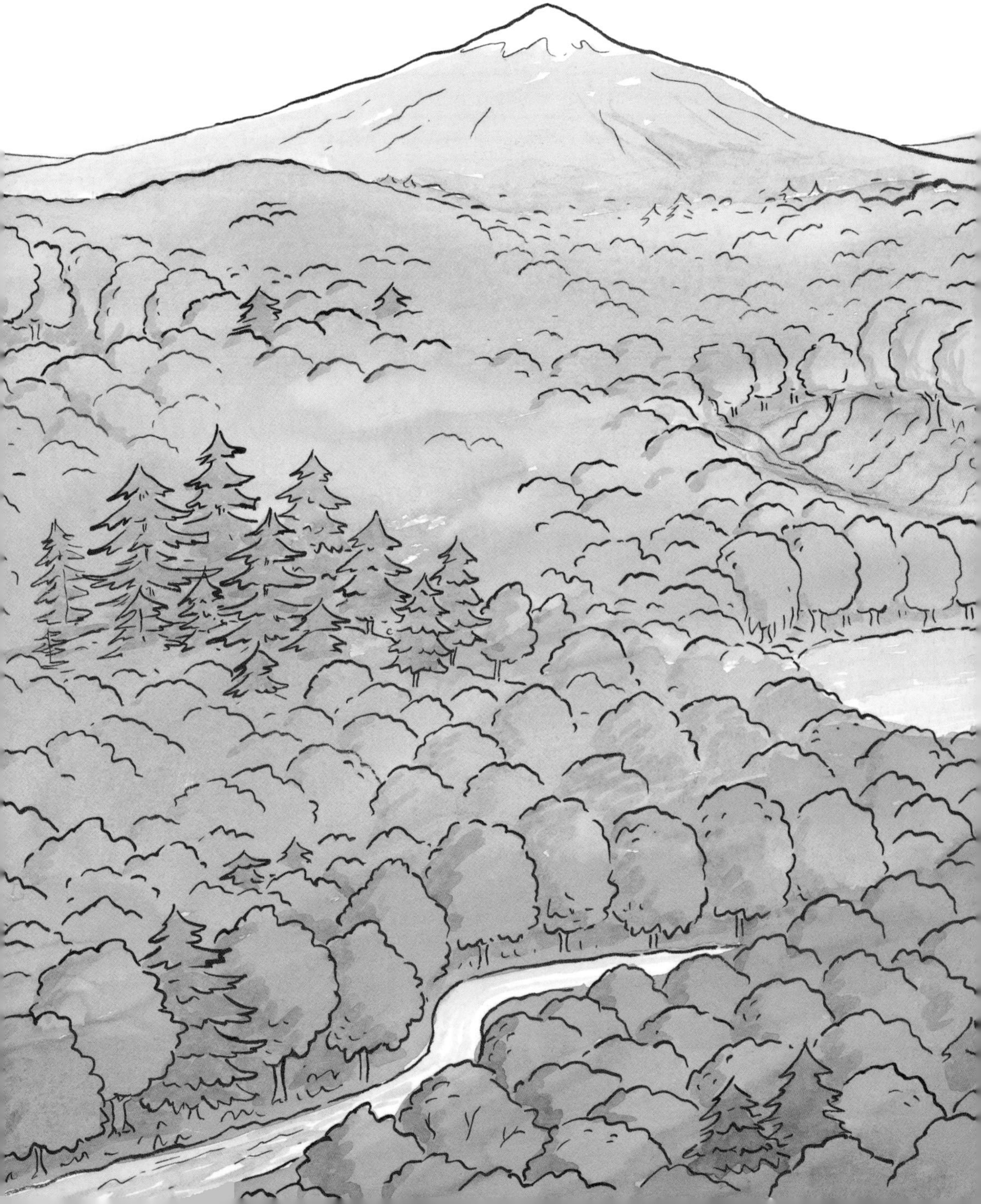

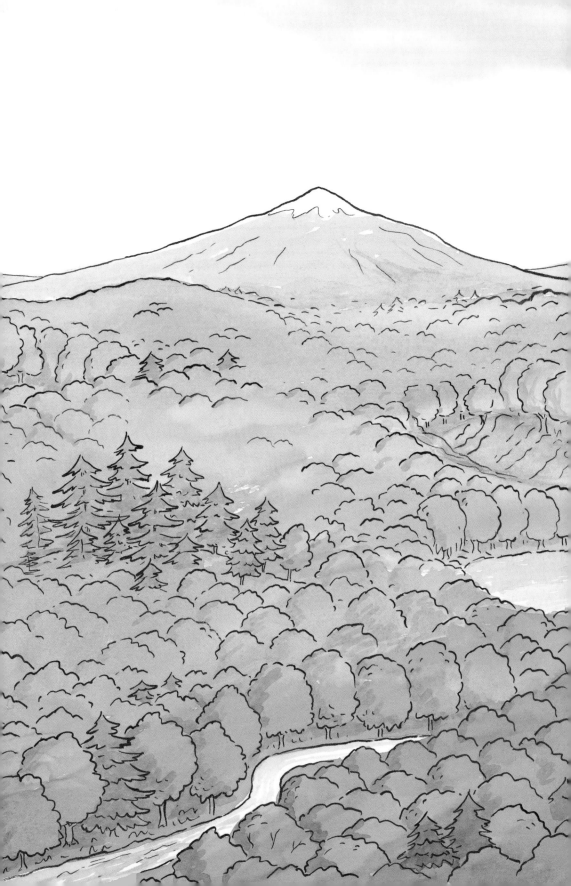

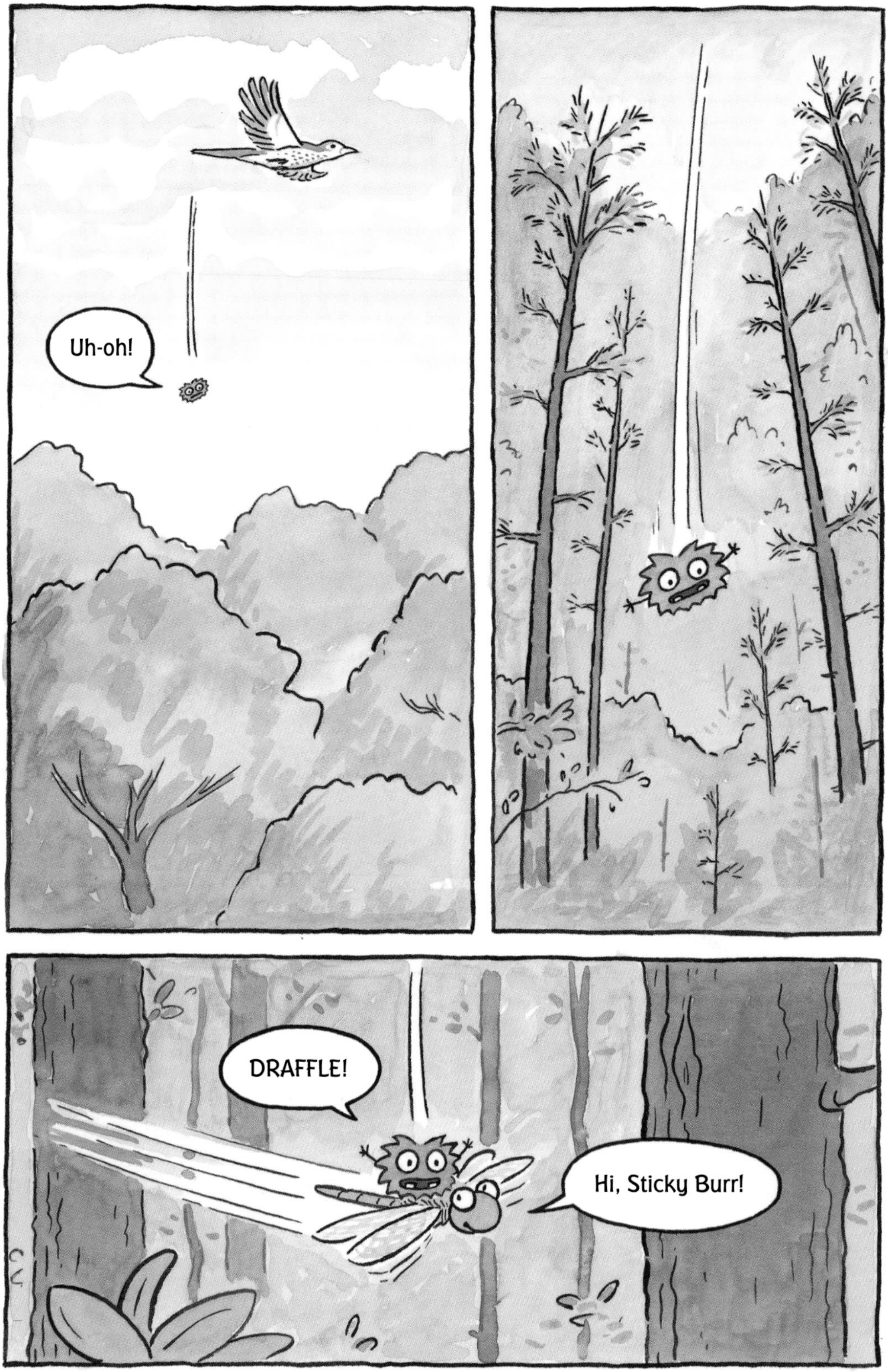
Uh-oh!
DRAFFLE!
Hi, Sticky Burr!

INSECTS I HAVE KNOWN

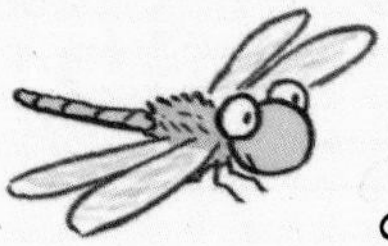

Draffle is a dragonfly, and my best friend. There are lots of insects in Burrwood Forest, and you'll see all of them if you look carefully enough.

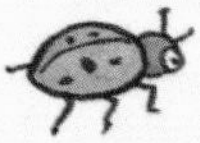

Ladybug

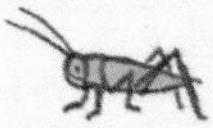

Cricket

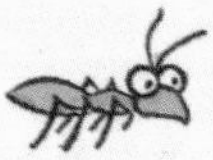

Ant

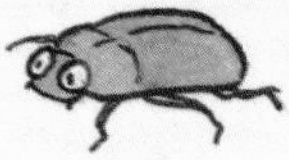

Beetle

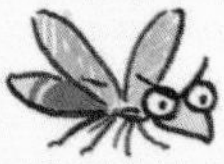

Wasp

(DANGEROUS!)

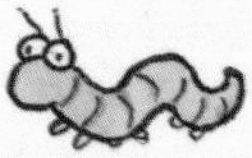

Caterpillar

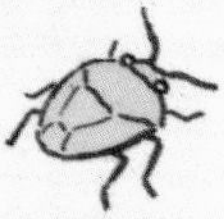

Stinkbug

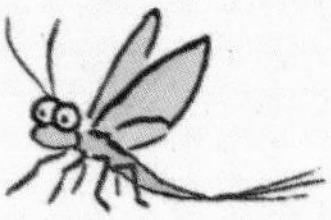

Mayfly

Grasshoppers are nimble and strong. Mossy Burr takes karate lessons from a grasshopper.

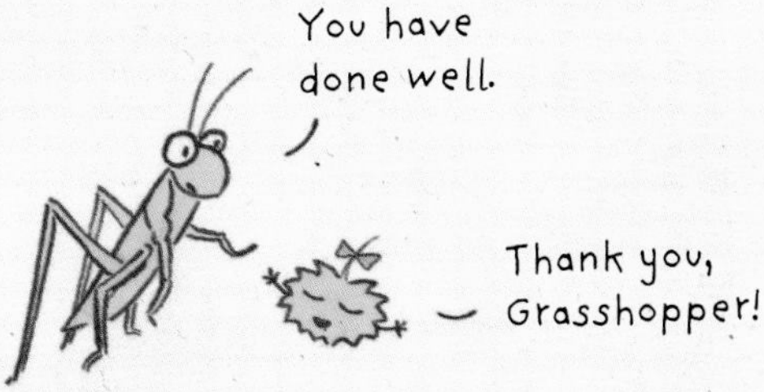
You have done well.
Thank you, Grasshopper!

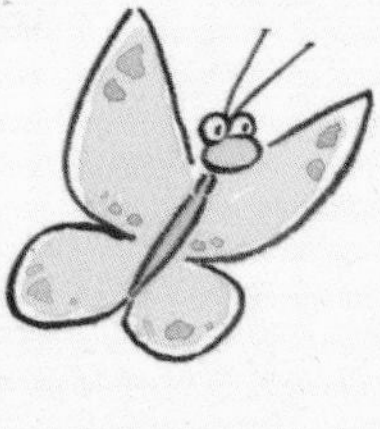

Butterflies are like royalty. They don't talk much—just flutter around looking grand. Some folks say they can grant wishes.

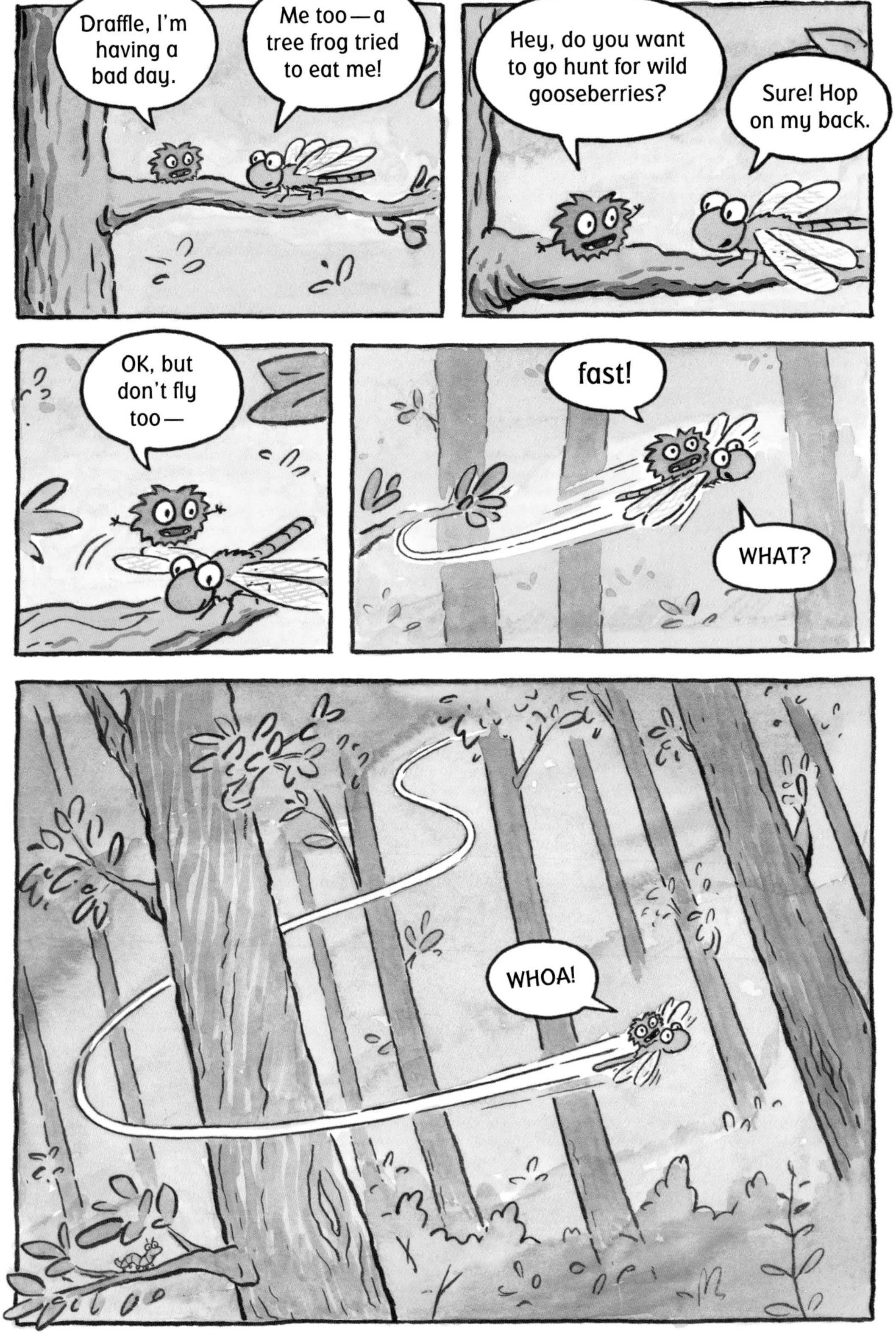

Draffle, I'm having a bad day.
Me too — a tree frog tried to eat me!
Hey, do you want to go hunt for wild gooseberries?
Sure! Hop on my back.
OK, but don't fly too —
fast!
WHAT?
WHOA!

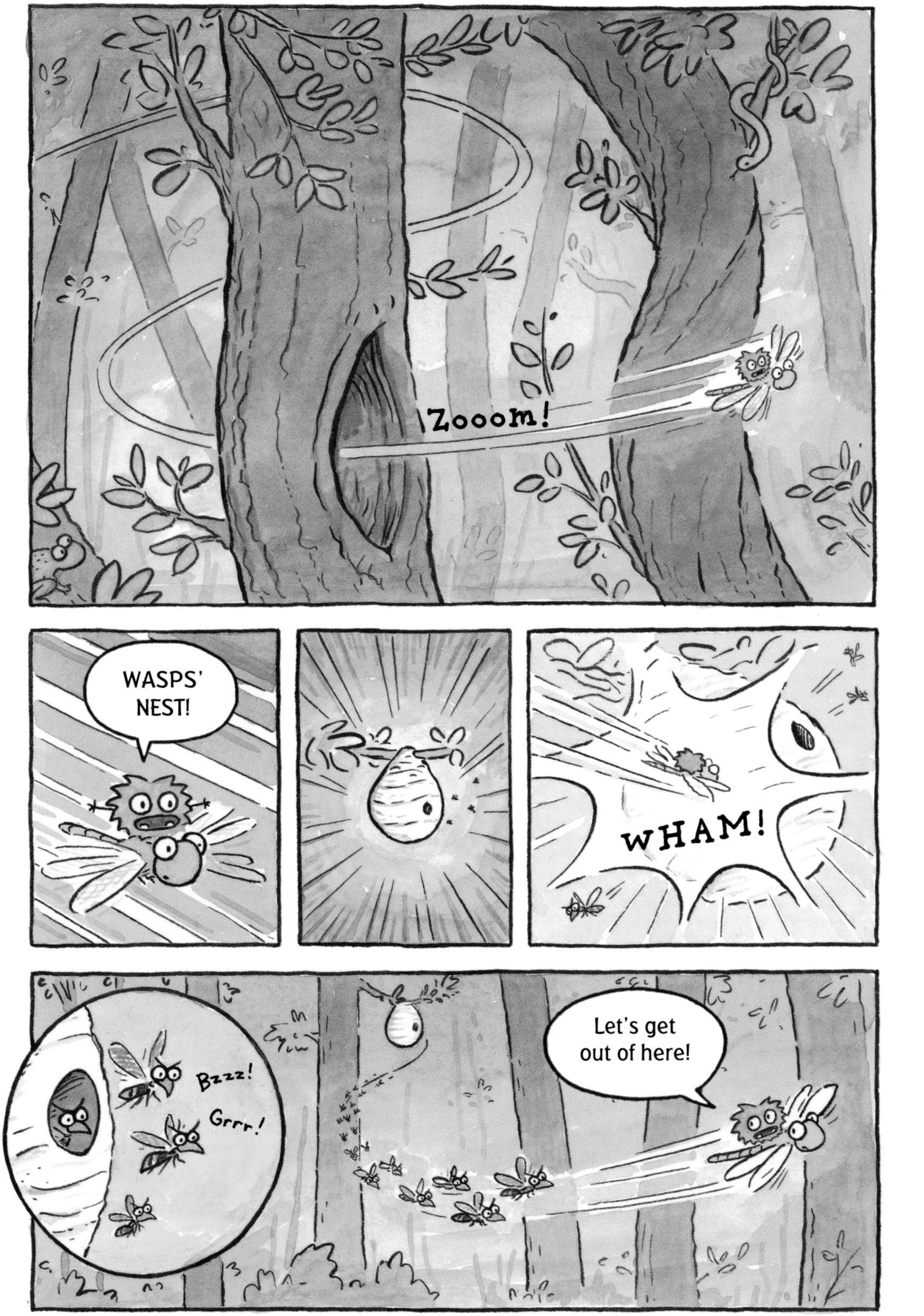
Zoooom!
WASPS' NEST!
WHAM!
Bzzz!
Grrr!
Let's get out of here!

DANGERS IN THE FOREST

Wasps are the most dangerous insects in Burrwood Forest. Mossy Burr says to just be still and they will leave you alone. She is much braver than me.

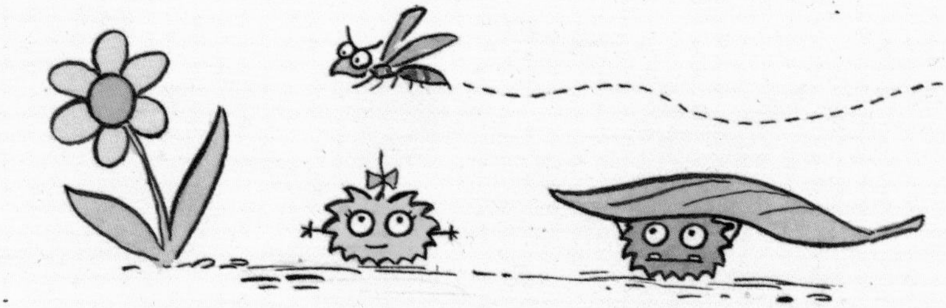

Here are more creatures to avoid:

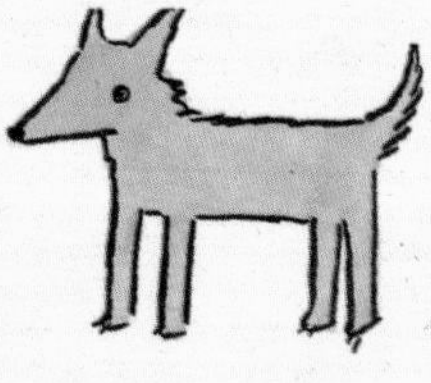

Wild Dogs

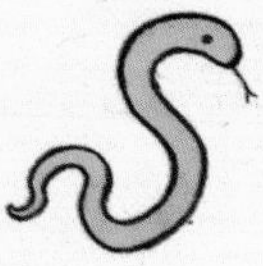

Snakes

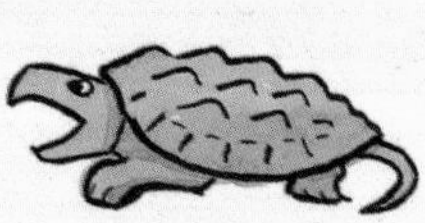

Snapping Turtles

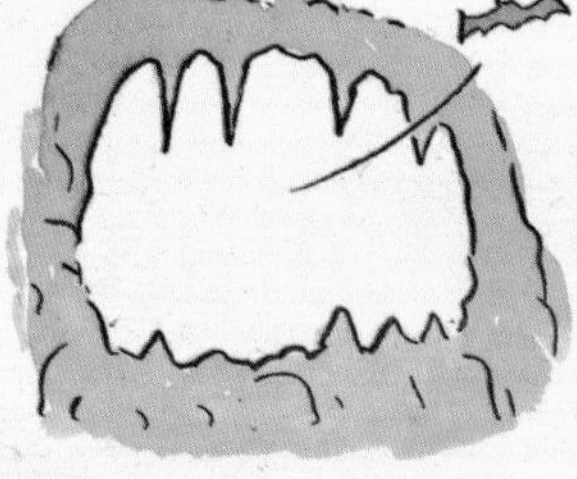

There are also dangerous places in the forest, like Gravel Gorge and Craggy Cave. If you ever visit Burrwood Forest, try to avoid them.

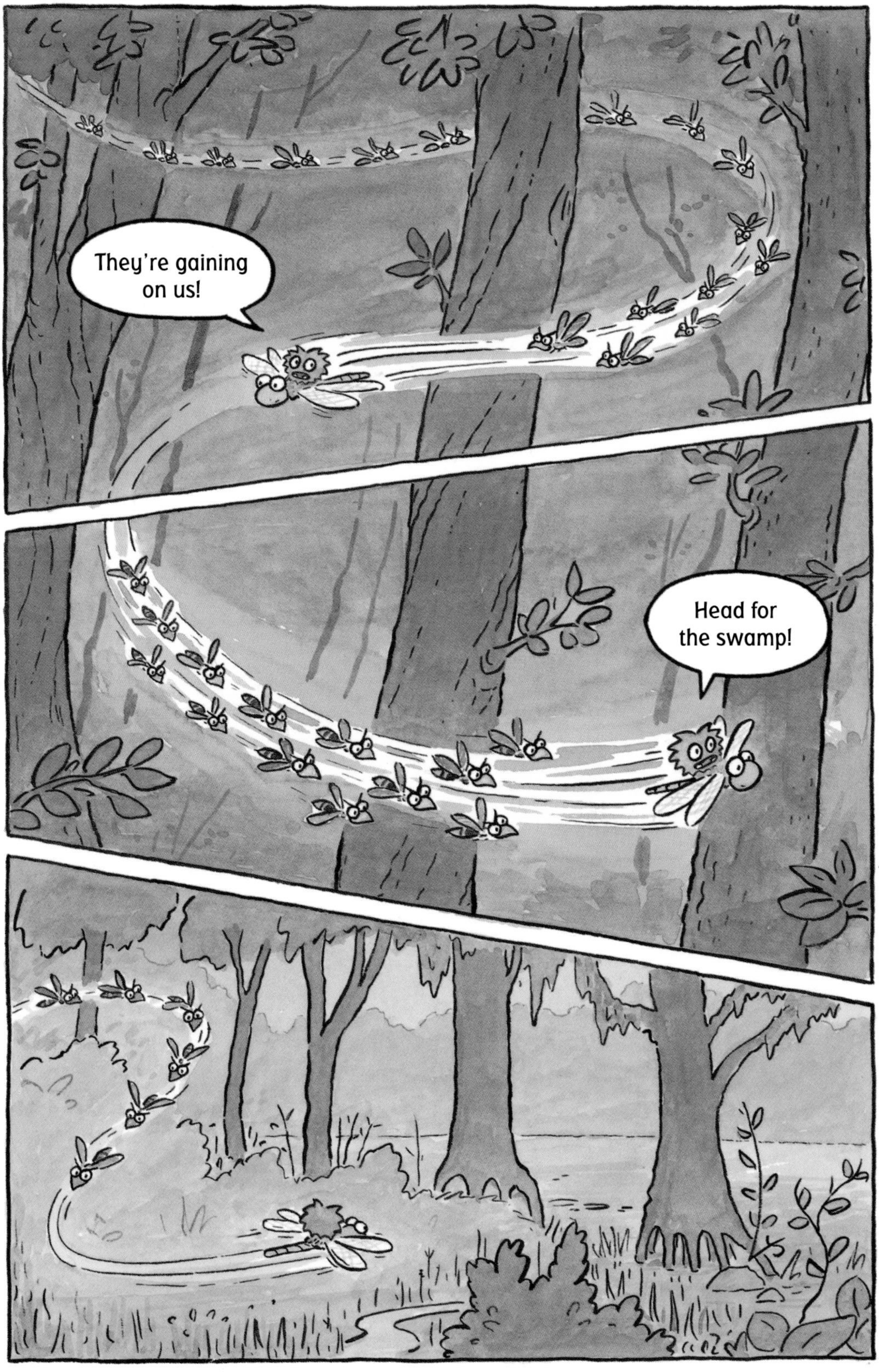
They're gaining on us!
Head for the swamp!

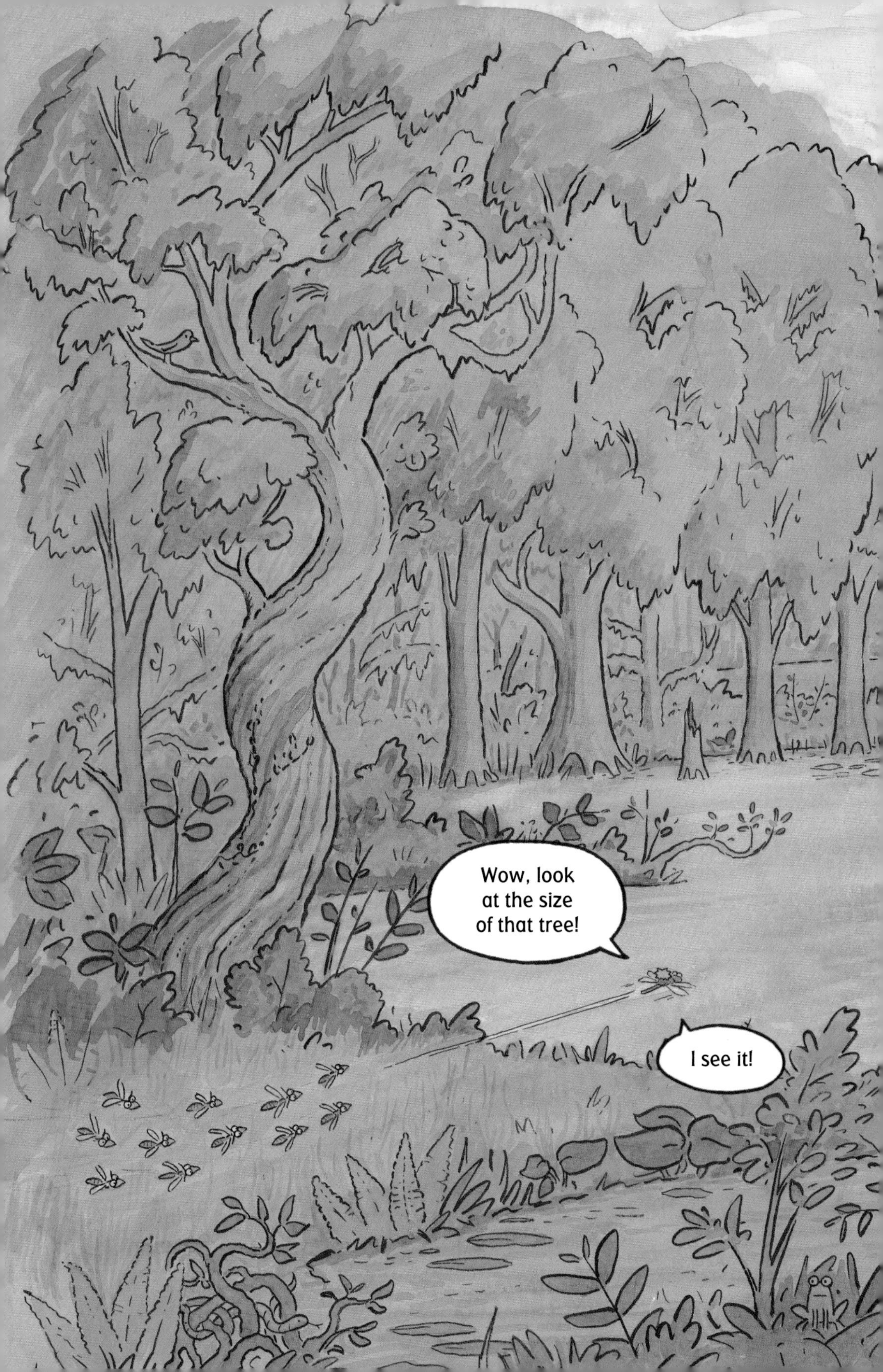
Wow, look at the size of that tree!
I see it!

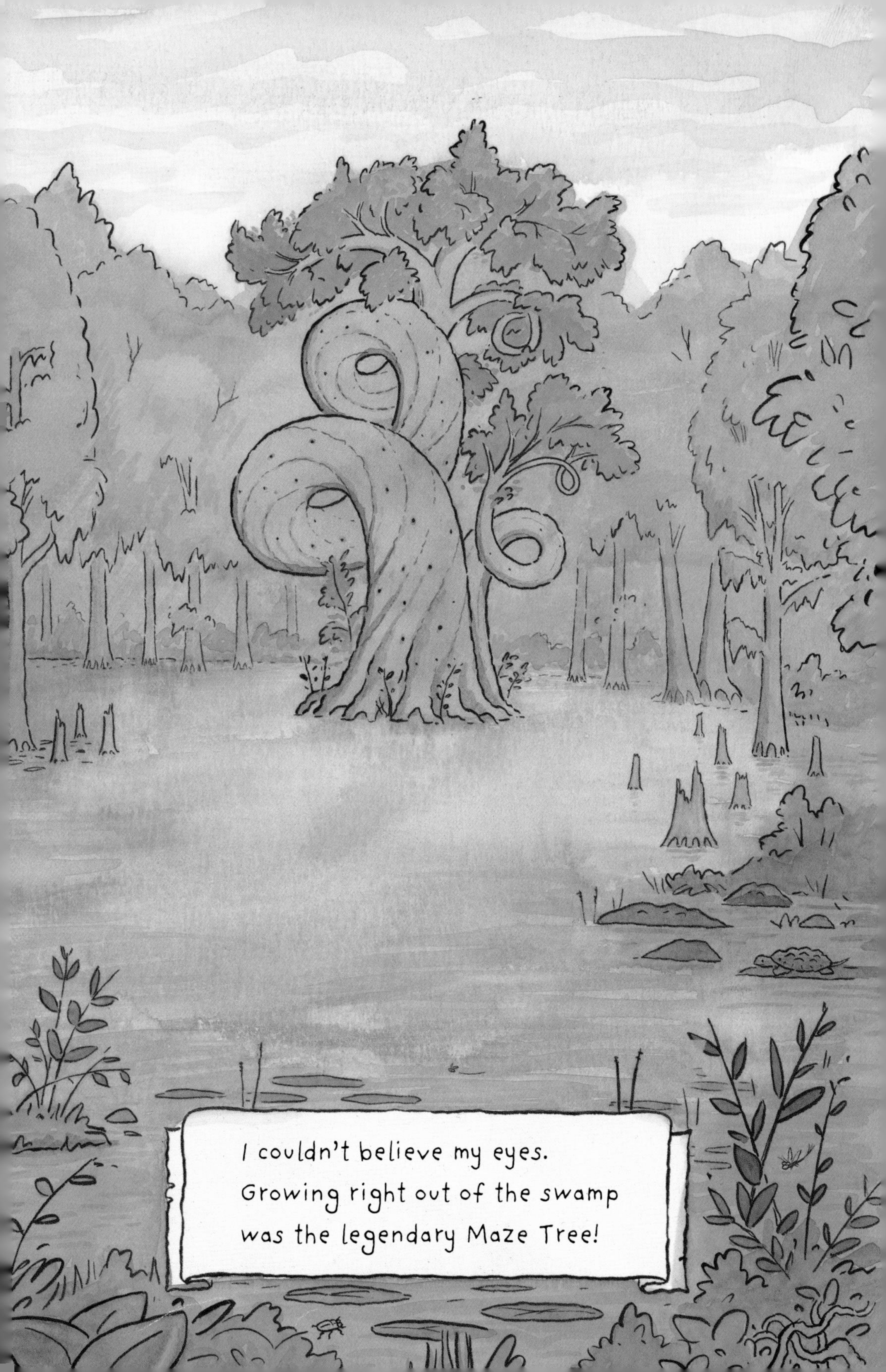
I couldn't believe my eyes.
Growing right out of the swamp
was the legendary Maze Tree!

THE MAZE TREE

My friend Walking Stick had told me about the Maze Tree, the most unusual tree in Burrwood Forest. It is filled with winding tunnels, and if you get lost in one, it is nearly impossible to find your way out!

Yum!

Walking Stick is an expert on trees—how they look, how they grow, how they taste. He even looks like a tree himself!

There are many other interesting trees in the forest, but none as strange or mysterious as the Maze Tree.

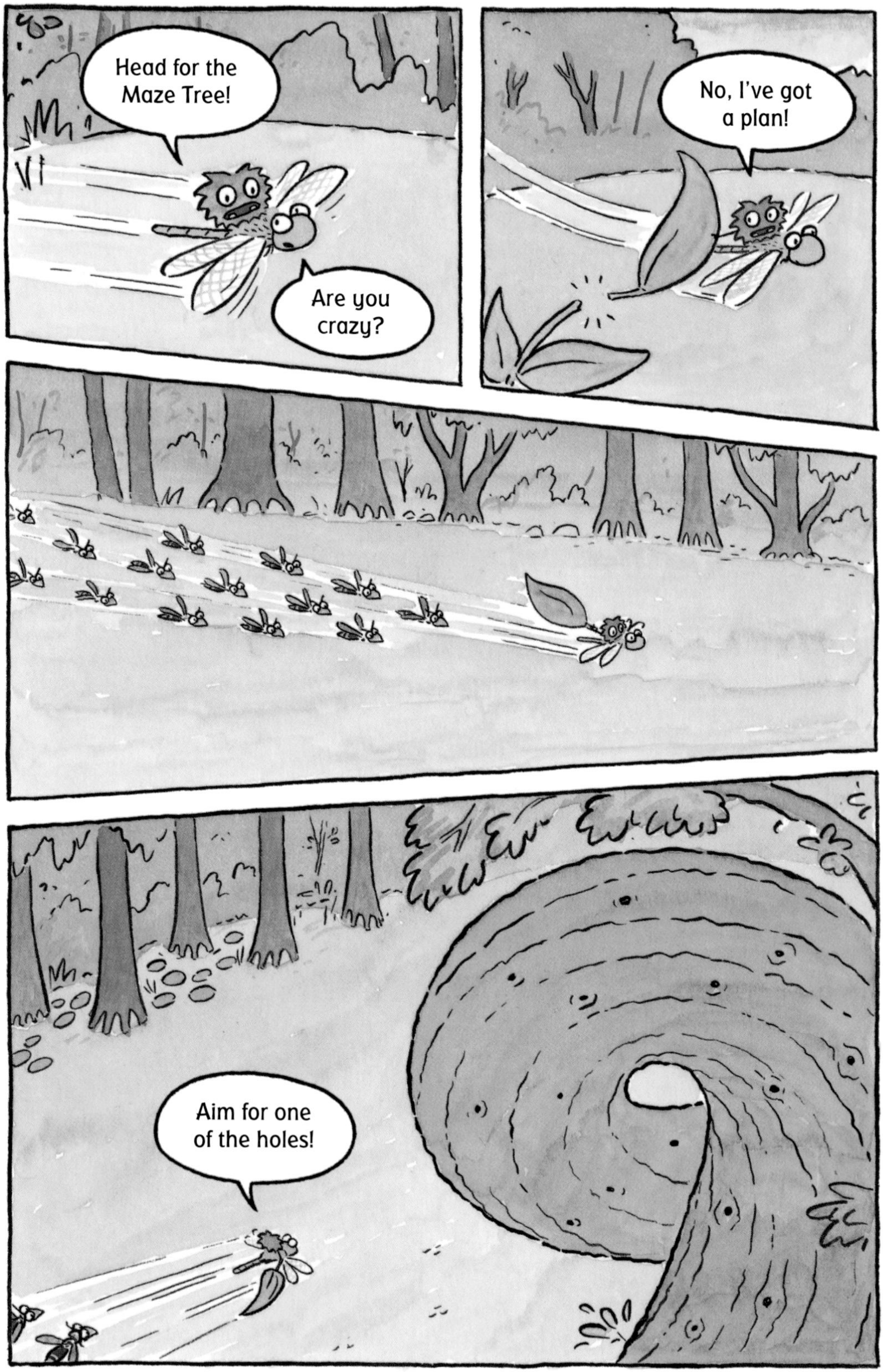
Head for the Maze Tree!
Are you crazy?
No, I've got a plan!
Aim for one of the holes!

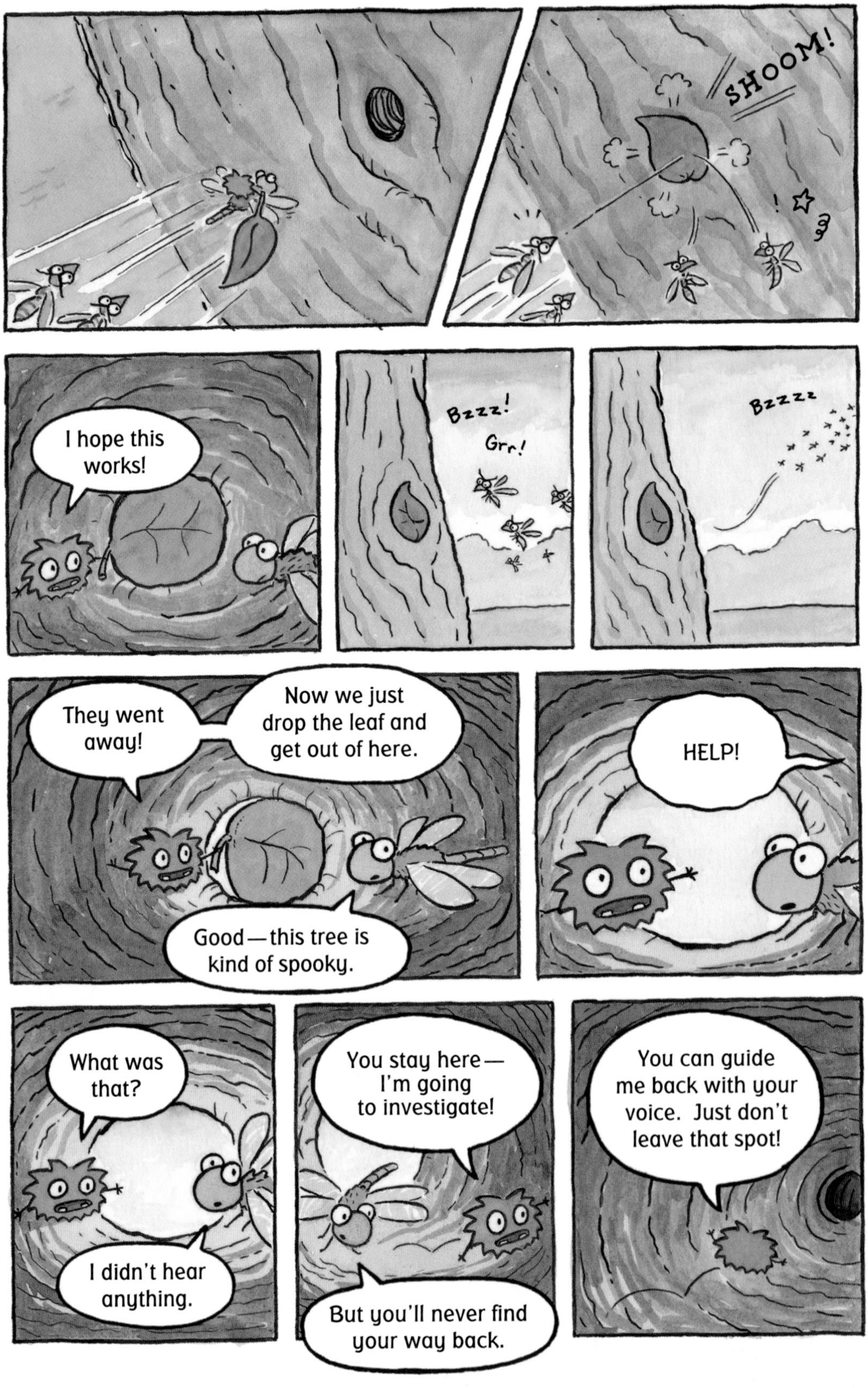
SHOOM!
I hope this works!
Bzzz!
Grr!
Bzzzz
They went away!
Now we just drop the leaf and get out of here.
Good—this tree is kind of spooky.
HELP!
What was that?
I didn't hear anything.
You stay here— I'm going to investigate!
But you'll never find your way back.
You can guide me back with your voice. Just don't leave that spot!

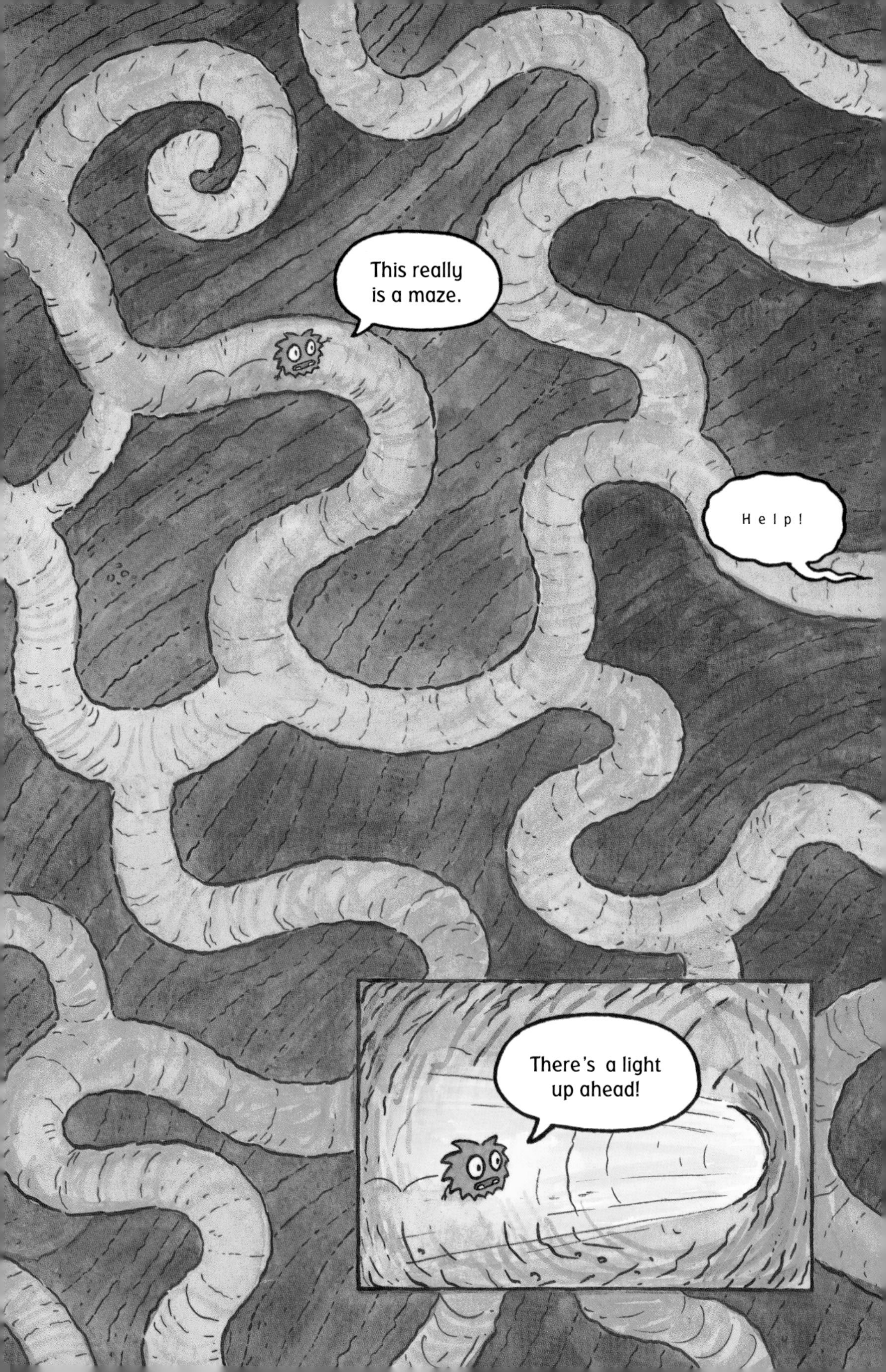
This really is a maze.
Help!
There's a light up ahead!

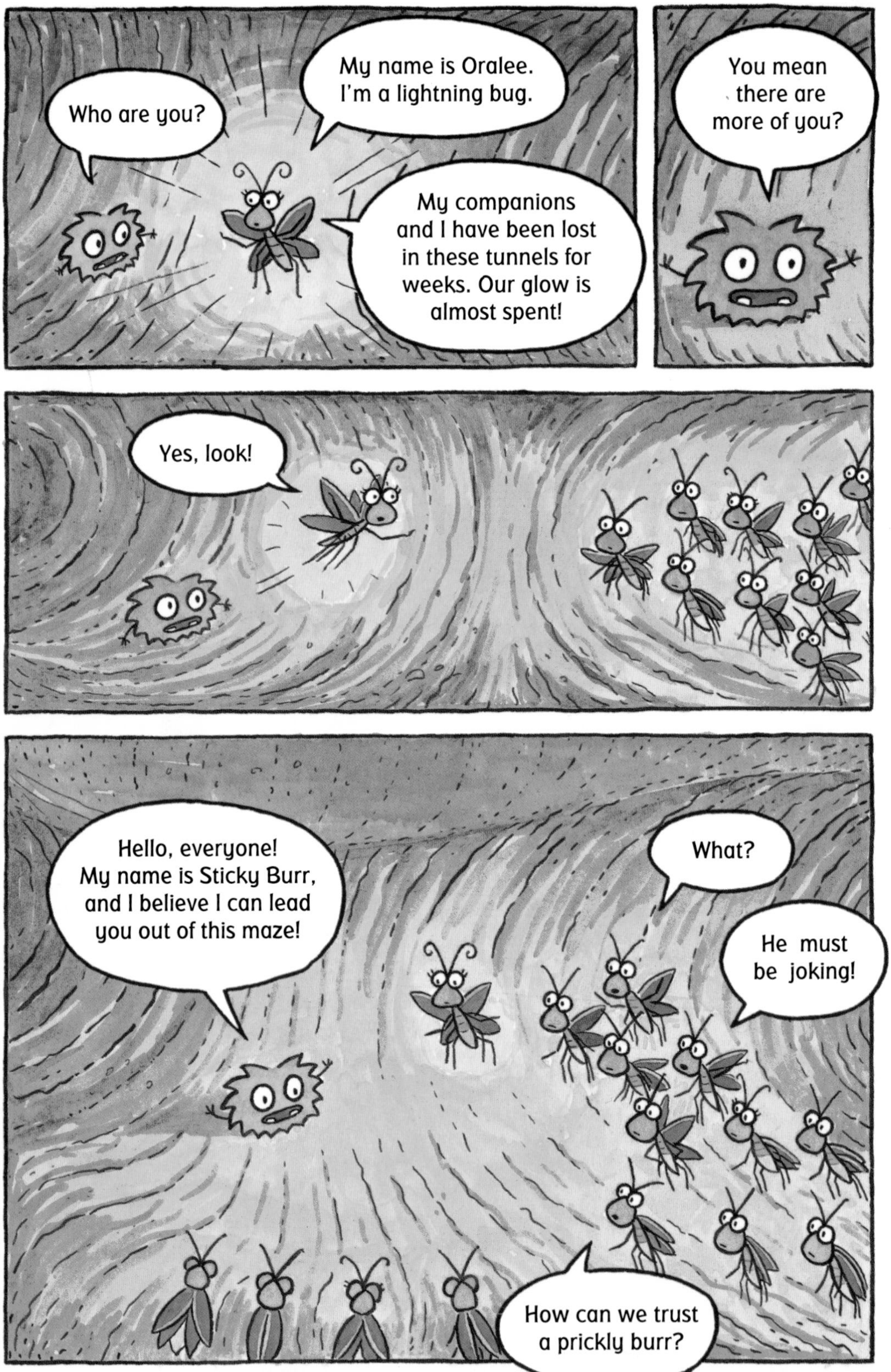
Who are you?
My name is Oralee. I'm a lightning bug.
My companions and I have been lost in these tunnels for weeks. Our glow is almost spent!
You mean there are more of you?
Yes, look!
Hello, everyone! My name is Sticky Burr, and I believe I can lead you out of this maze!
What?
He must be joking!
How can we trust a prickly burr?

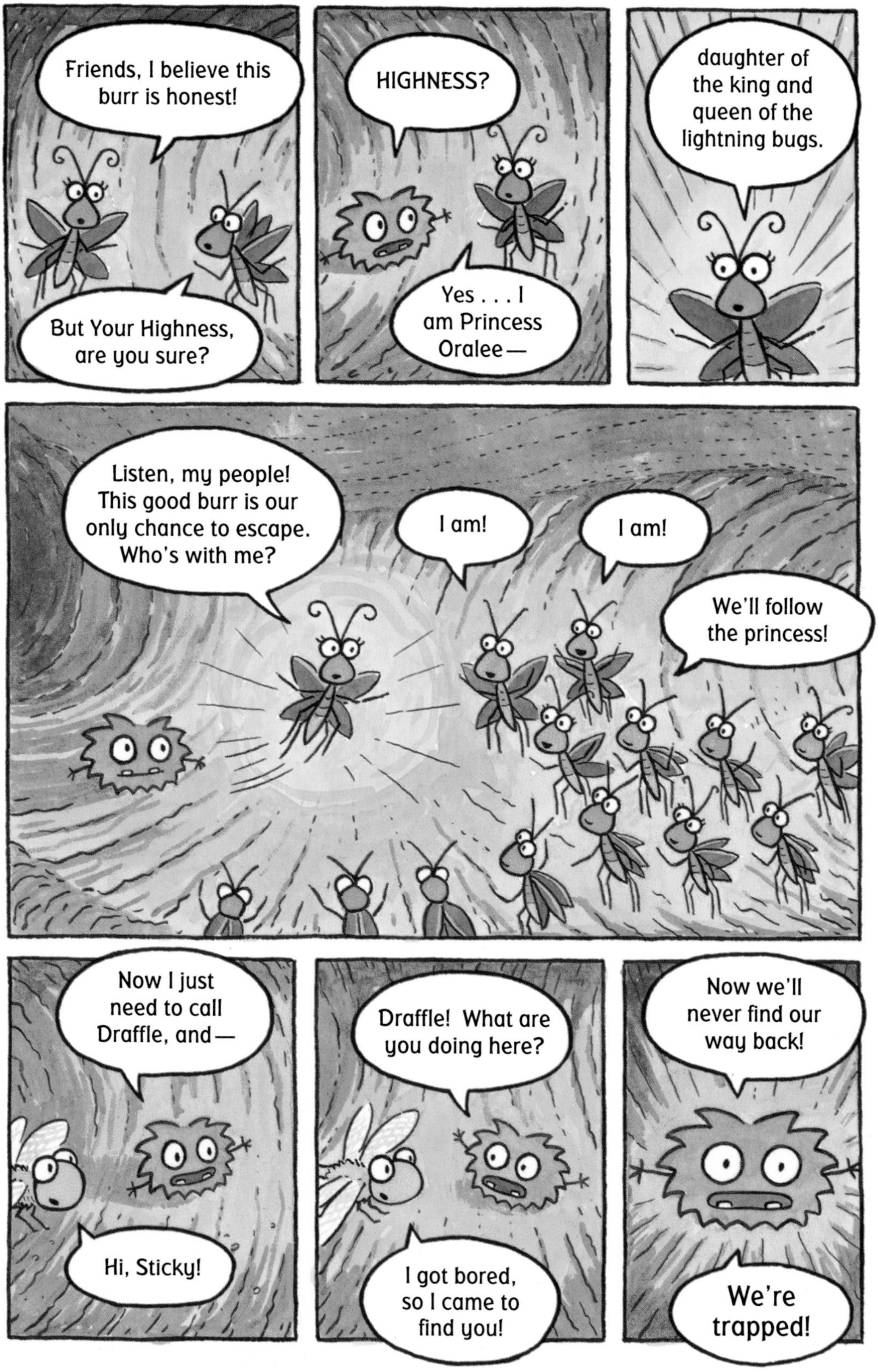
Friends, I believe this burr is honest!
But Your Highness, are you sure?
HIGHNESS?
Yes . . . I am Princess Oralee—
daughter of the king and queen of the lightning bugs.
Listen, my people! This good burr is our only chance to escape. Who's with me?
I am!
I am!
We'll follow the princess!
Now I just need to call Draffle, and—
Hi, Sticky!
Draffle! What are you doing here?
I got bored, so I came to find you!
Now we'll never find our way back!
We're trapped!

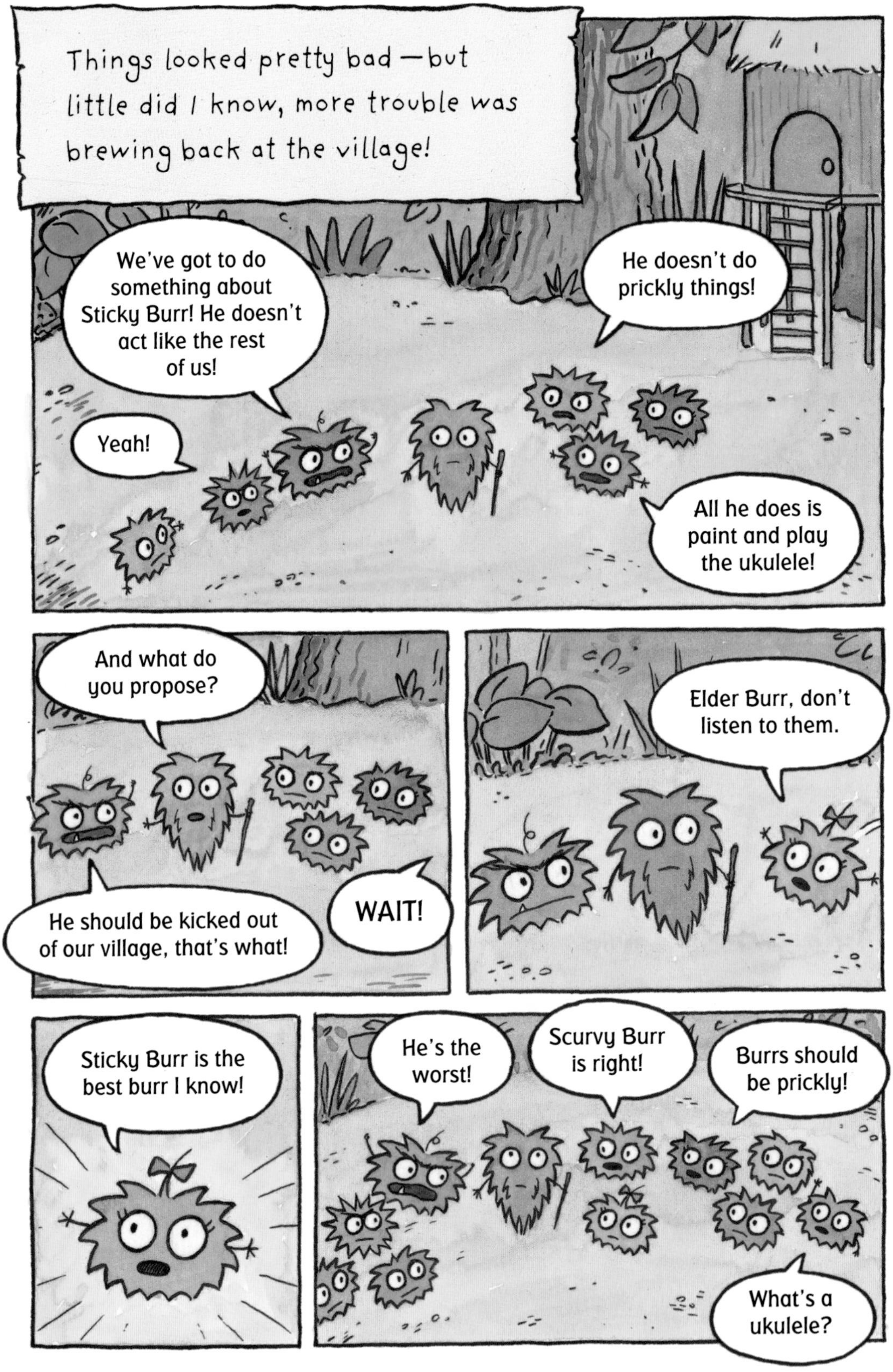
Things looked pretty bad—but little did I know, more trouble was brewing back at the village!
We've got to do something about Sticky Burr! He doesn't act like the rest of us!
Yeah!
He doesn't do prickly things!
All he does is paint and play the ukulele!
And what do you propose?
He should be kicked out of our village, that's what!
WAIT!
Elder Burr, don't listen to them.
Sticky Burr is the best burr I know!
He's the worst!
Scurvy Burr is right!
Burrs should be prickly!
What's a ukulele?

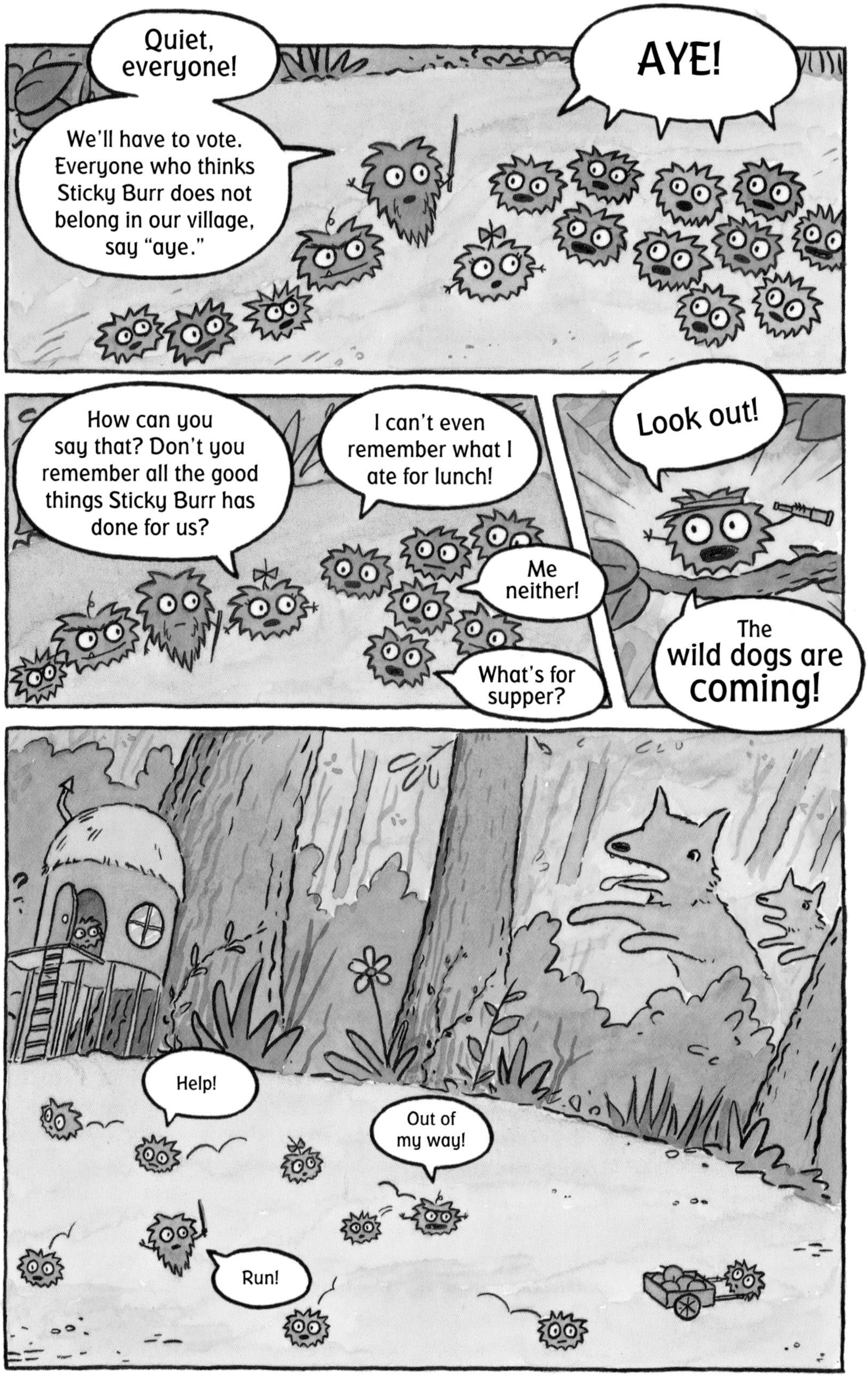
Quiet, everyone!
We'll have to vote. Everyone who thinks Sticky Burr does not belong in our village, say "aye."
AYE!
How can you say that? Don't you remember all the good things Sticky Burr has done for us?
I can't even remember what I ate for lunch!
Me neither!
What's for supper?
Look out!
The wild dogs are coming!
Help!
Out of my way!
Run!

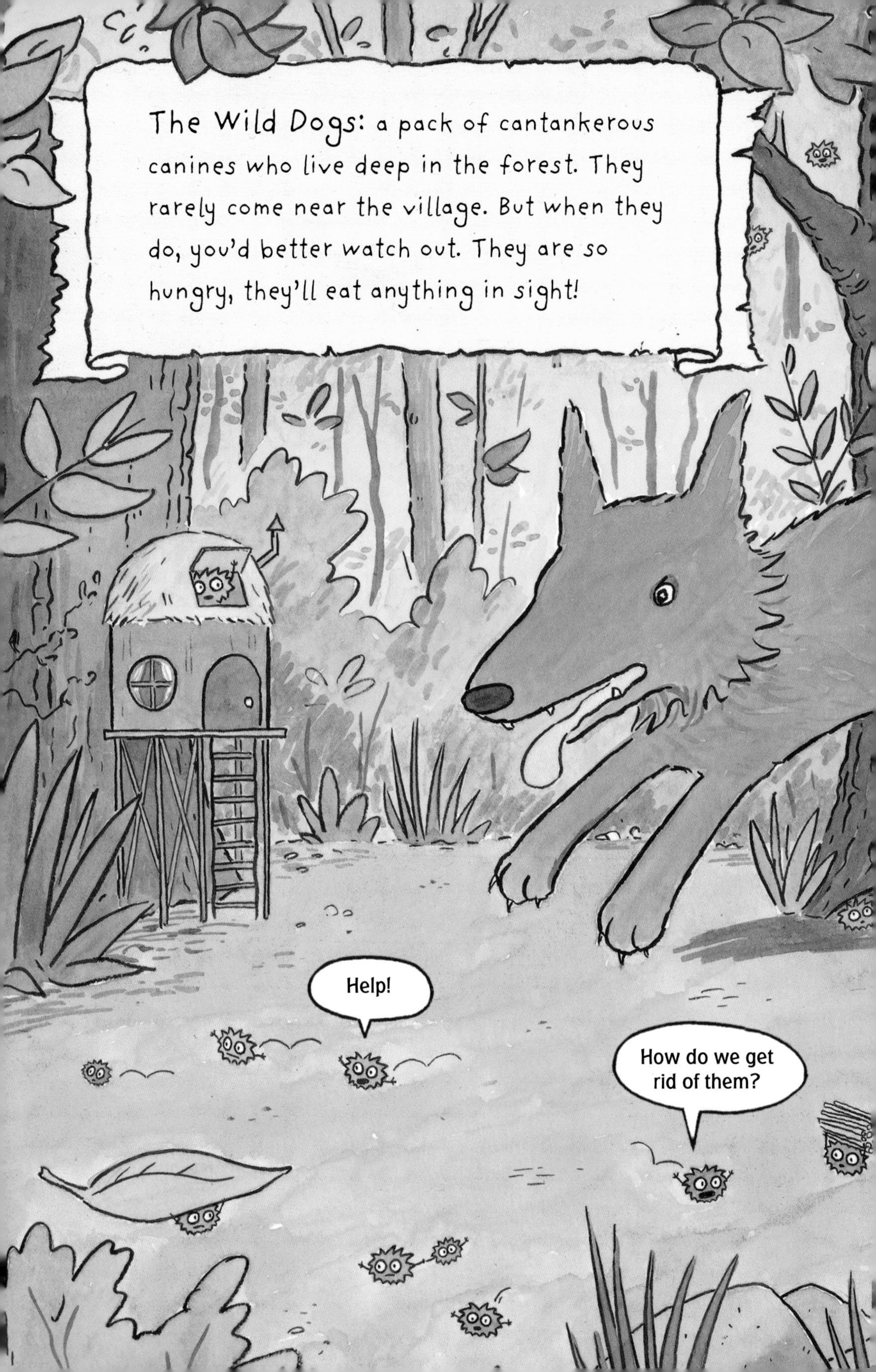
The Wild Dogs: a pack of cantankerous canines who live deep in the forest. They rarely come near the village. But when they do, you'd better watch out. They are so hungry, they'll eat anything in sight!
Help!
How do we get rid of them?

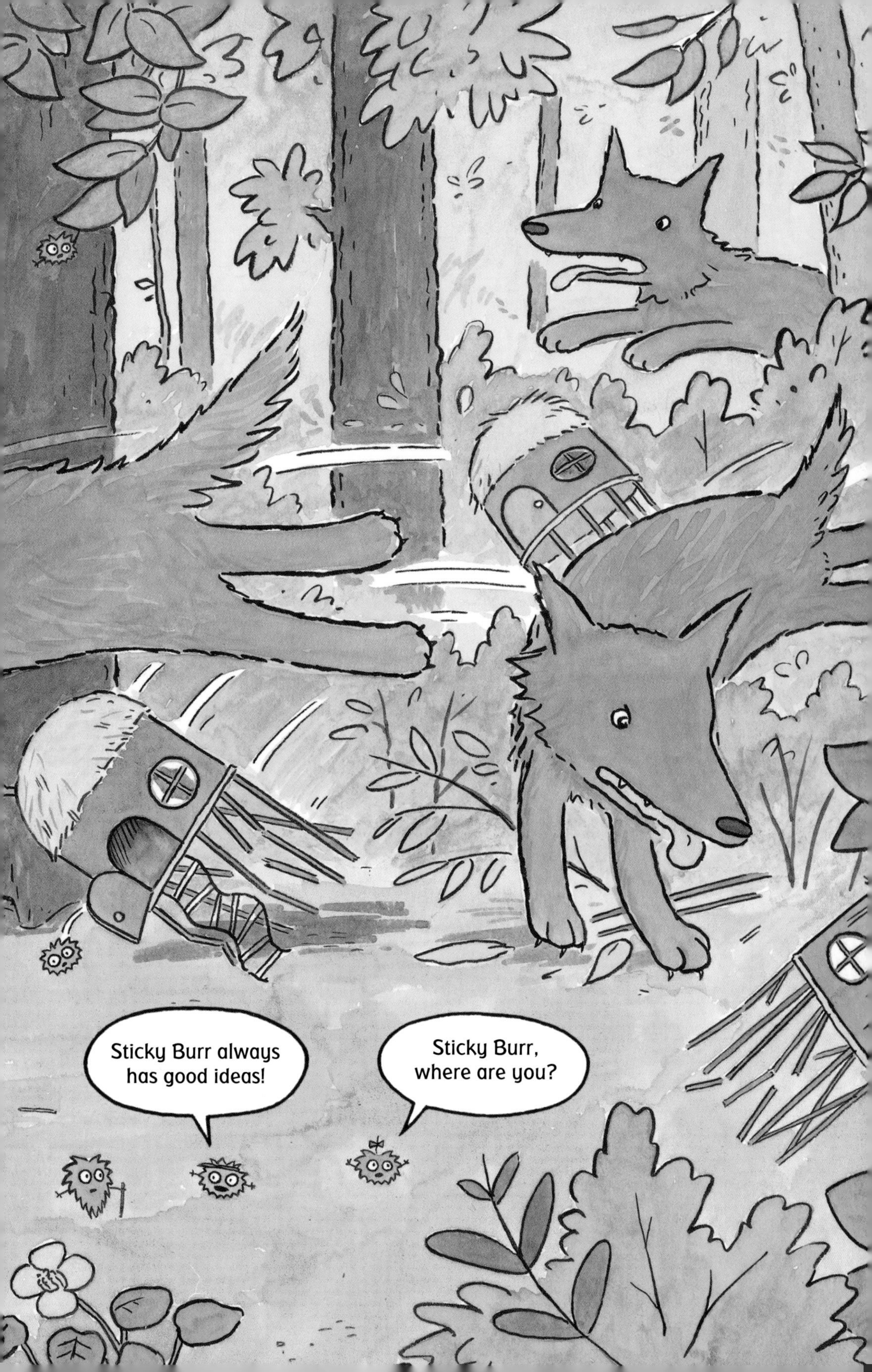
Sticky Burr always has good ideas!
Sticky Burr, where are you?

STICKY SITUATIONS

Life in Burrwood Forest can be dangerous,
and I've been in many sticky situations.
One time I got trapped on a branch during
the spring floods.

Hang on!

Another time, I got stuck
on the tail of a wild dog.

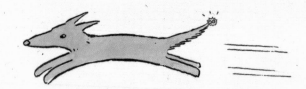

Finally he fell asleep, but it
took five burrs to pull me off!

Pull!

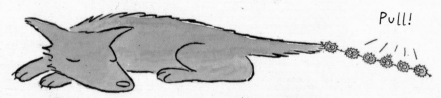

Once, I went into the forest to practice my ukulele and got stuck on a mossy tree.

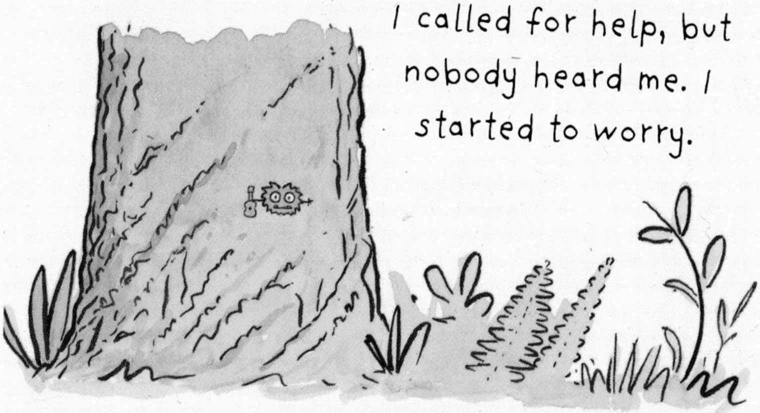

I called for help, but nobody heard me. I started to worry.

I made up a song to pass the time. It went like this:

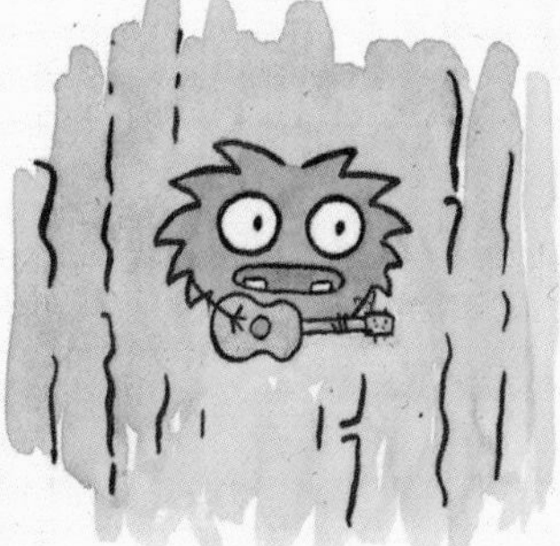

Stuck on a tree,
Stuck on a tree,
Won't somebody help me?
Life can be funny,
Strange as can be,
When you're stuck on a tree,
Like me!

Finally Draffle came along and pulled me off.

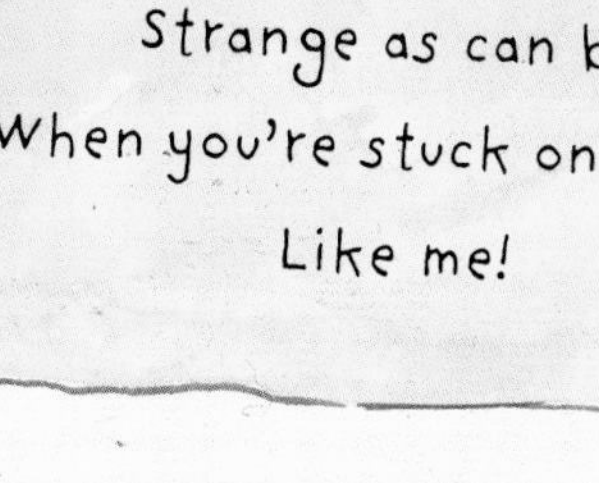
Thanks!

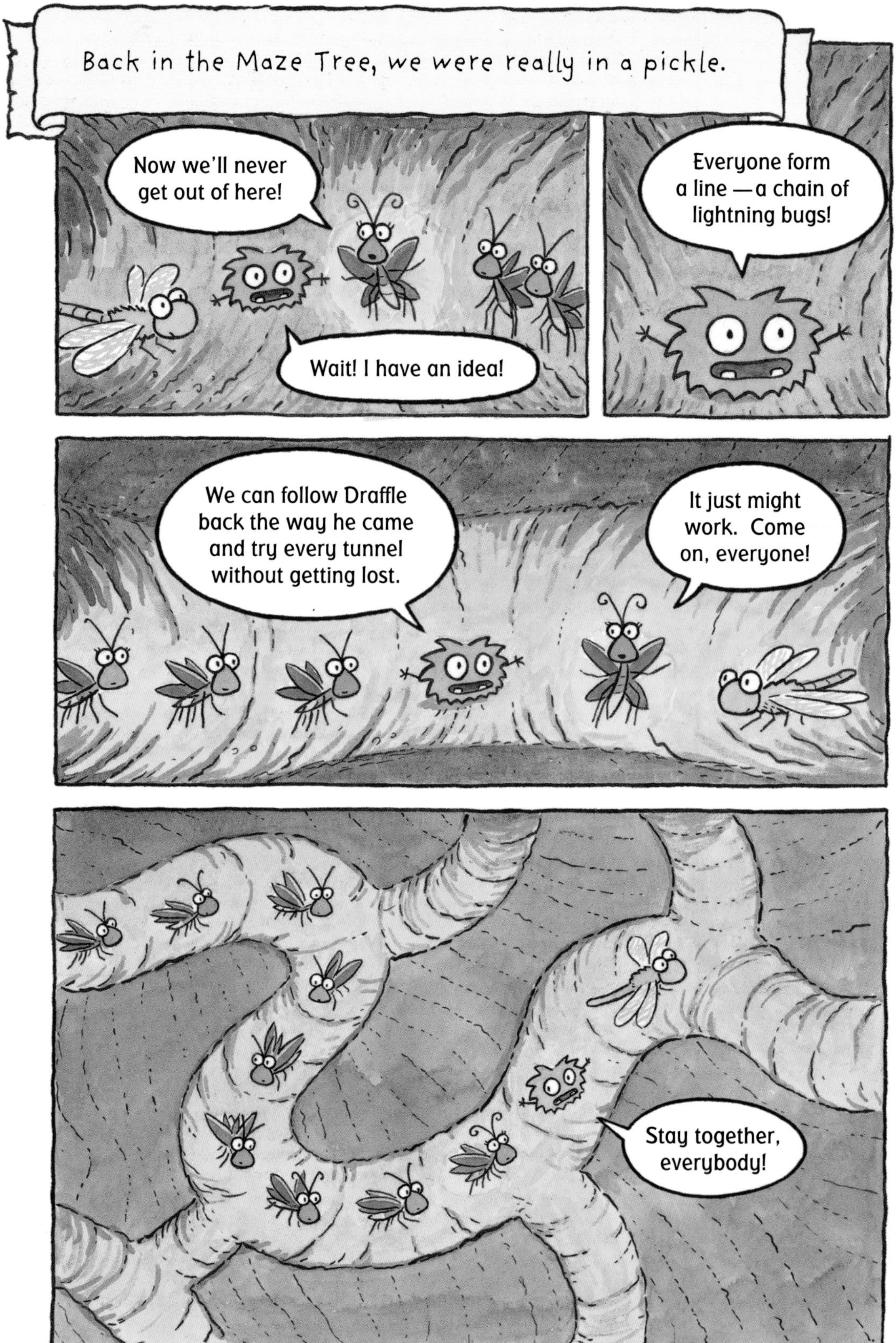
Back in the Maze Tree, we were really in a pickle.
Now we'll never get out of here!
Wait! I have an idea!
Everyone form a line — a chain of lightning bugs!
We can follow Draffle back the way he came and try every tunnel without getting lost.
It just might work. Come on, everyone!
Stay together, everybody!

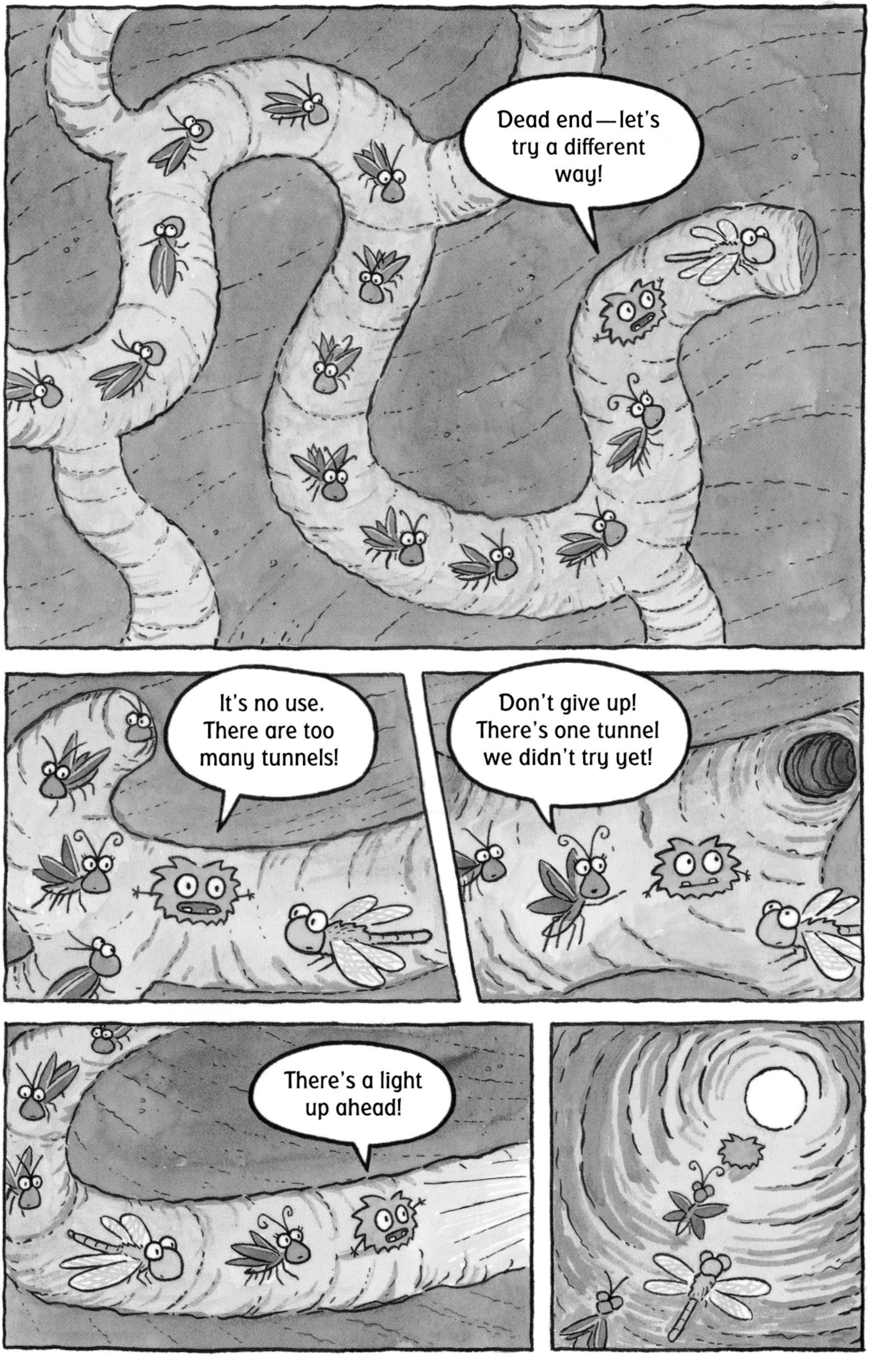
Dead end—let's try a different way!
It's no use. There are too many tunnels!
Don't give up! There's one tunnel we didn't try yet!
There's a light up ahead!

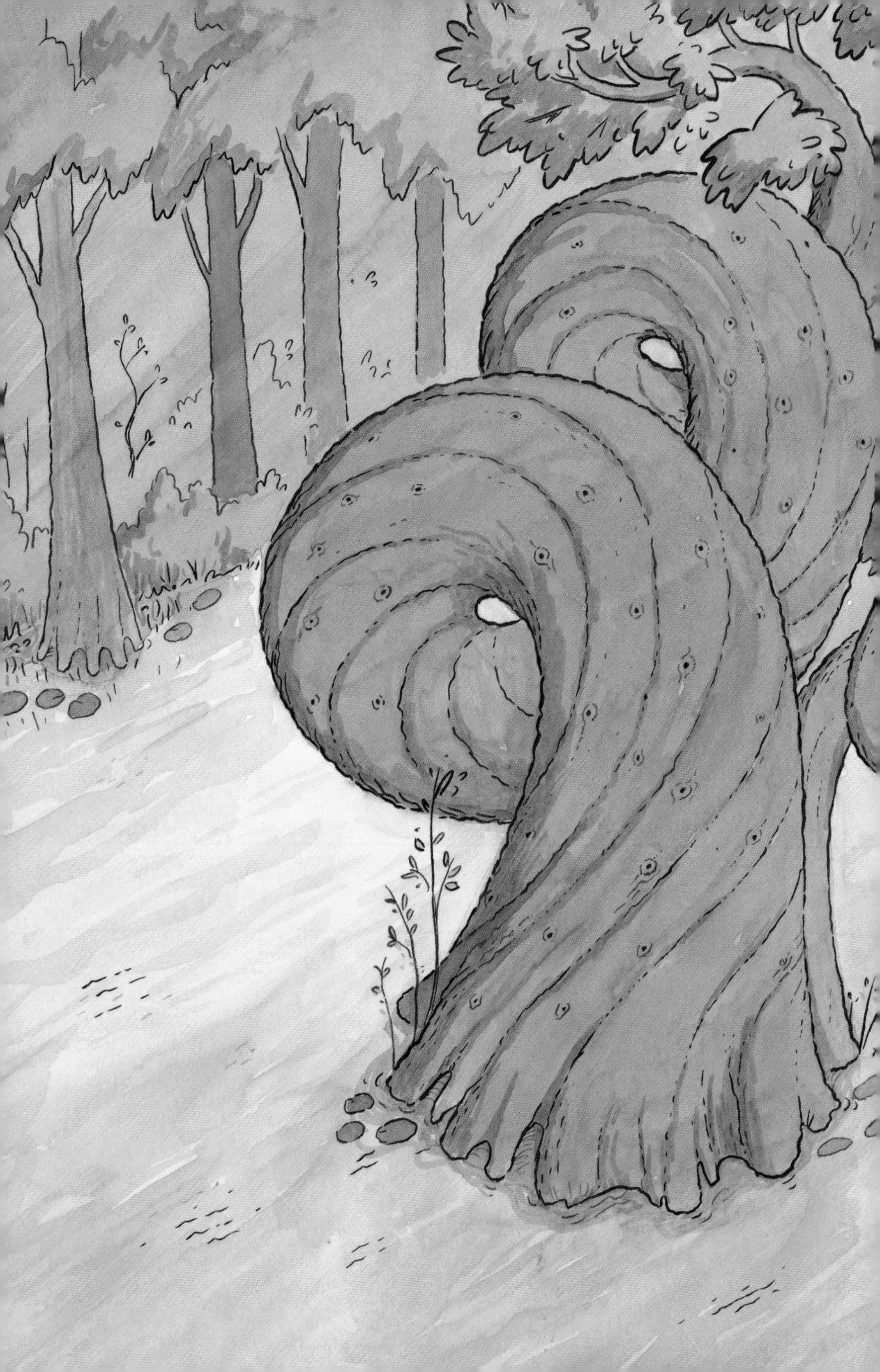

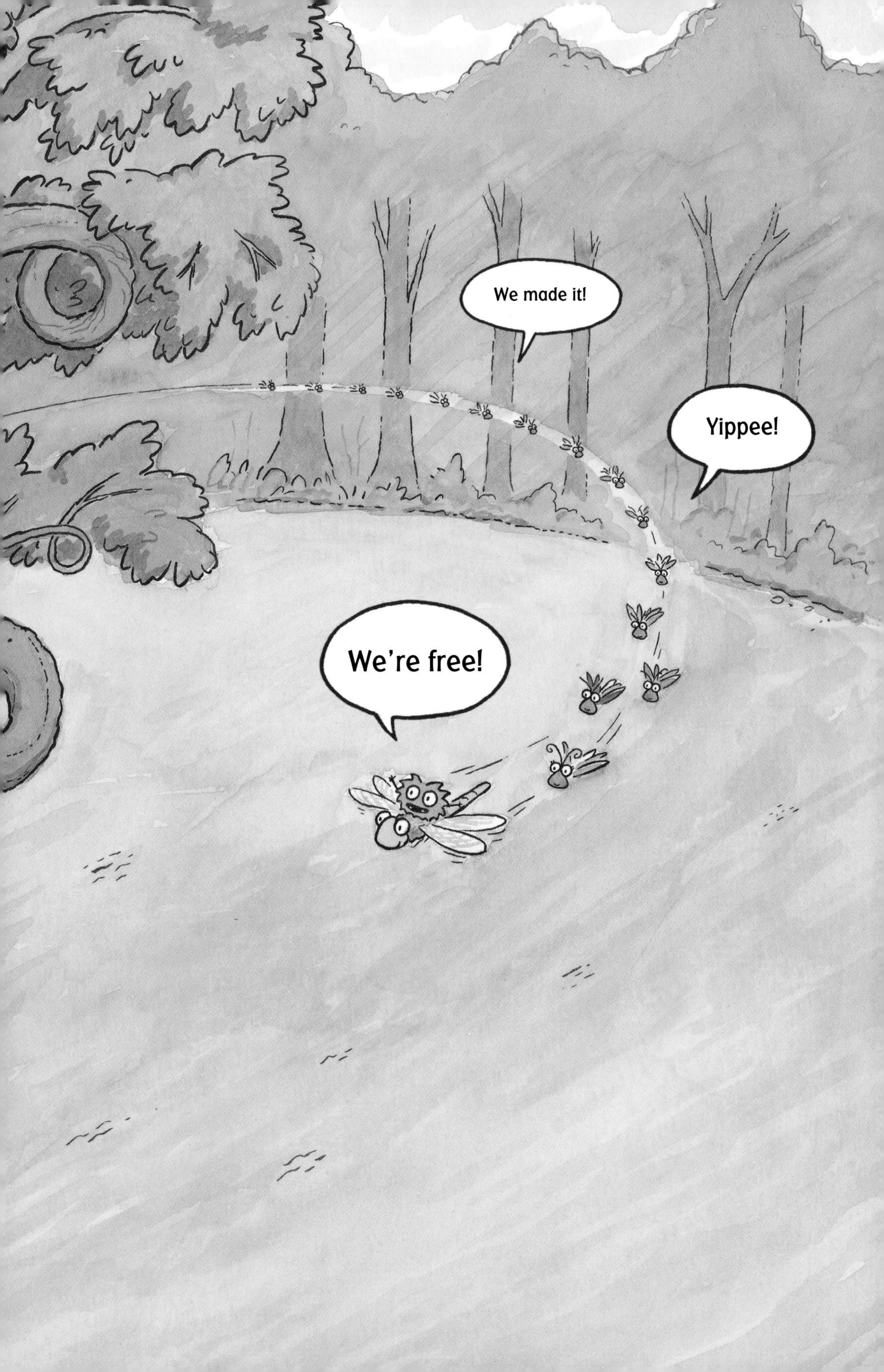
We made it!
Yippee!
We're free!

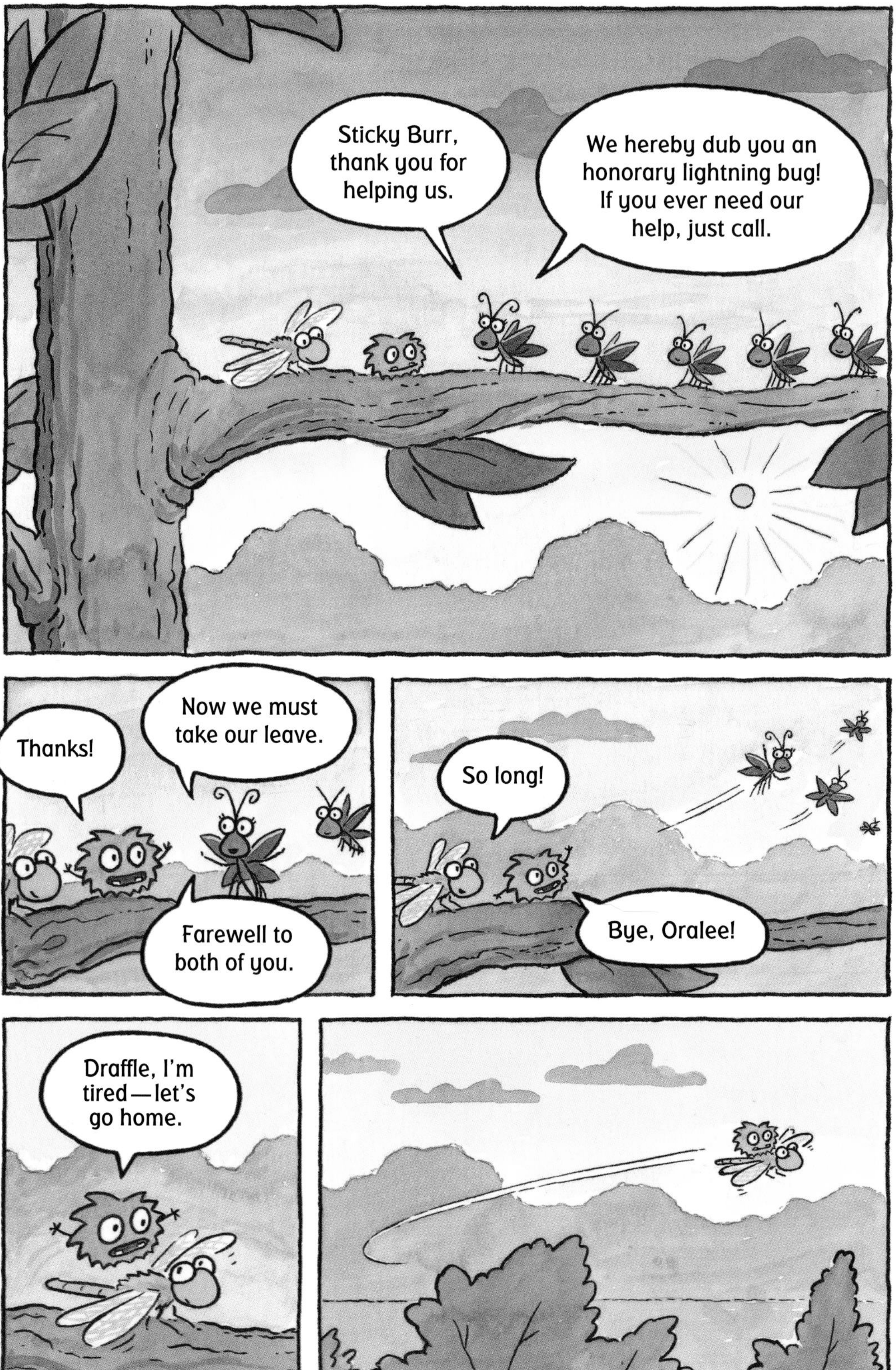
Sticky Burr, thank you for helping us.
We hereby dub you an honorary lightning bug! If you ever need our help, just call.
Thanks!
Now we must take our leave.
Farewell to both of you.
So long!
Bye, Oralee!
Draffle, I'm tired—let's go home.

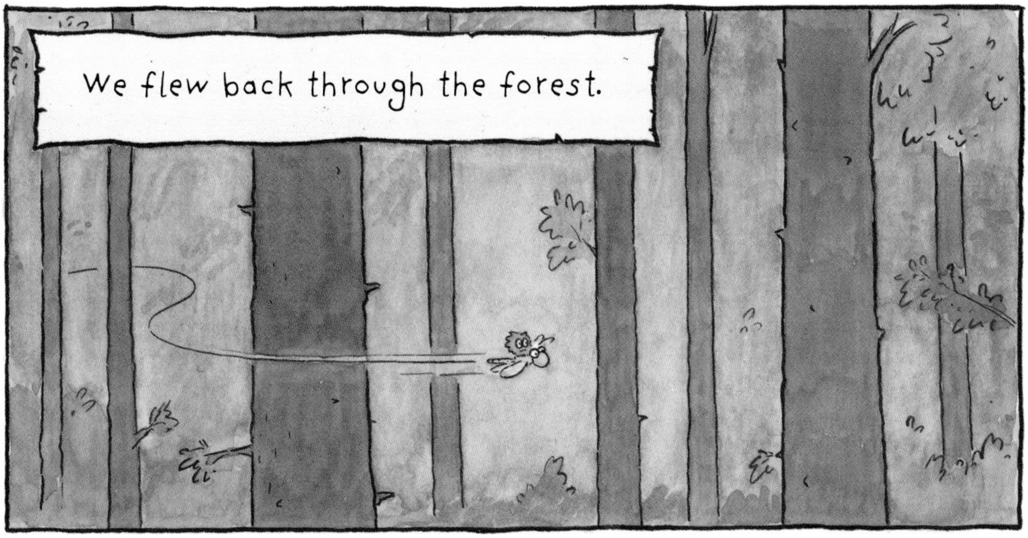
We flew back through the forest.

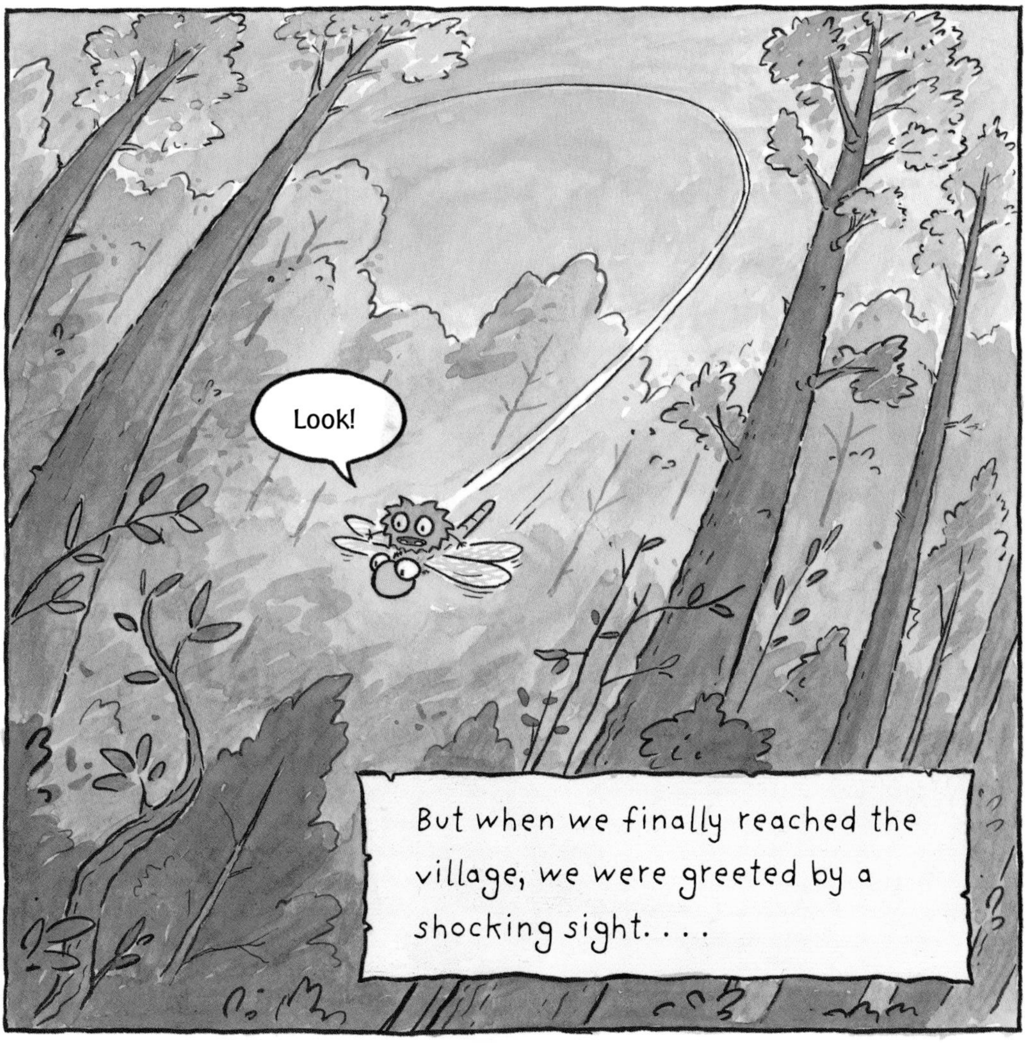
Look!
But when we finally reached the village, we were greeted by a shocking sight. . . .

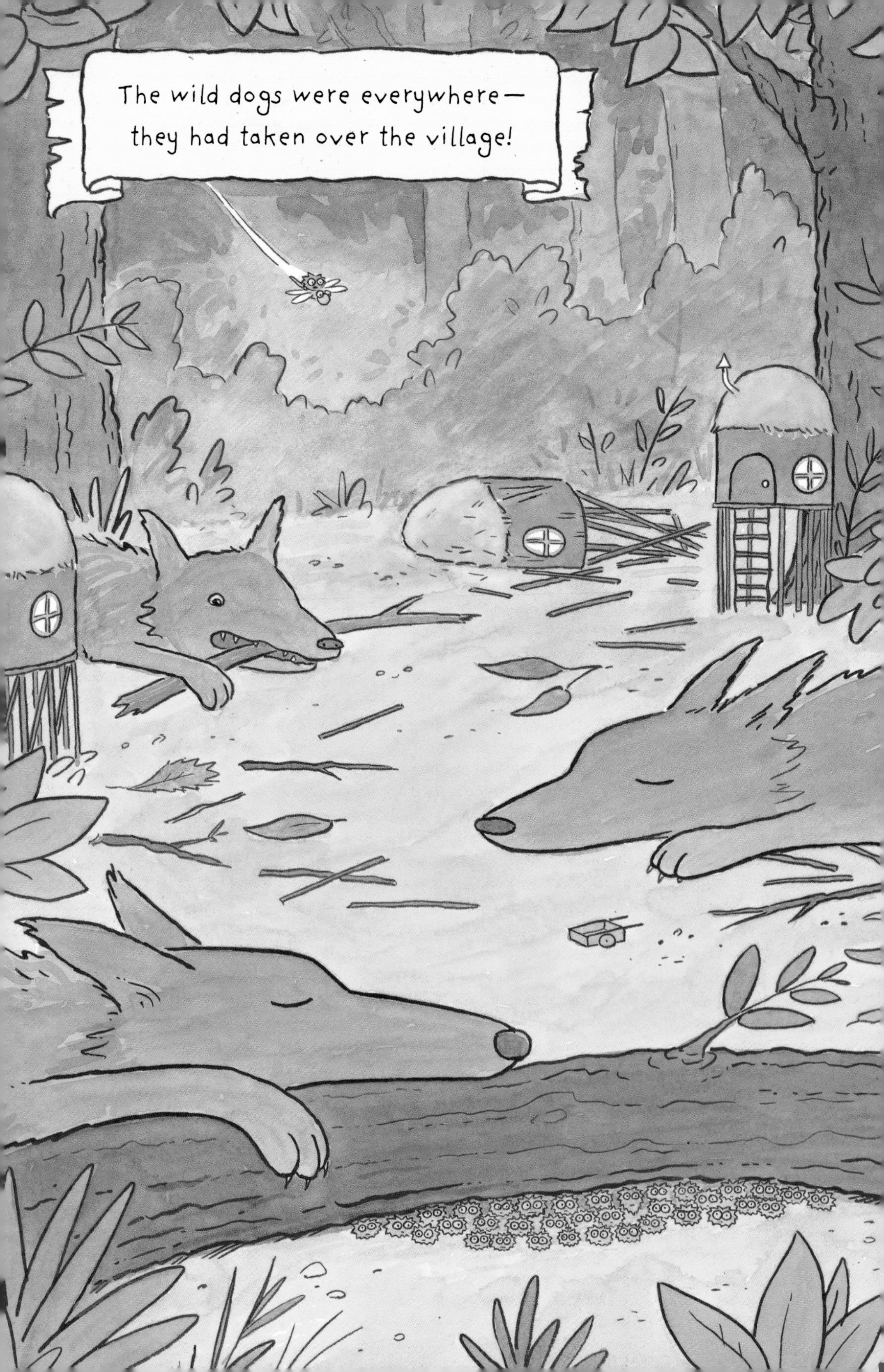
The wild dogs were everywhere—
they had taken over the village!

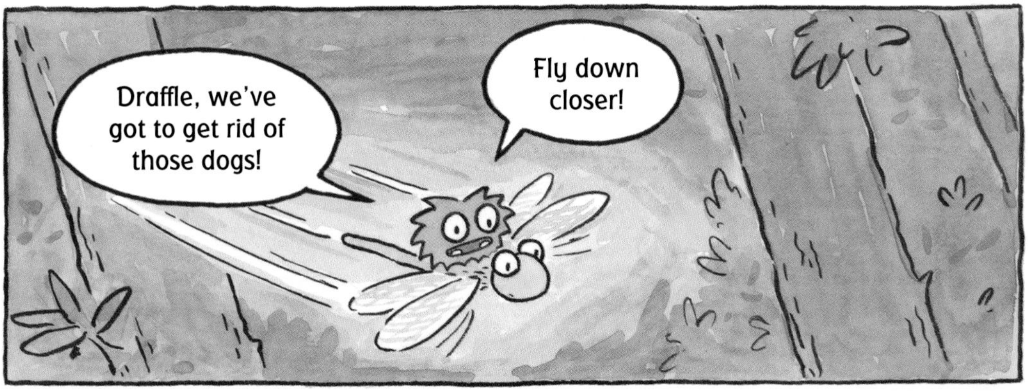
Draffle, we've got to get rid of those dogs!
Fly down closer!

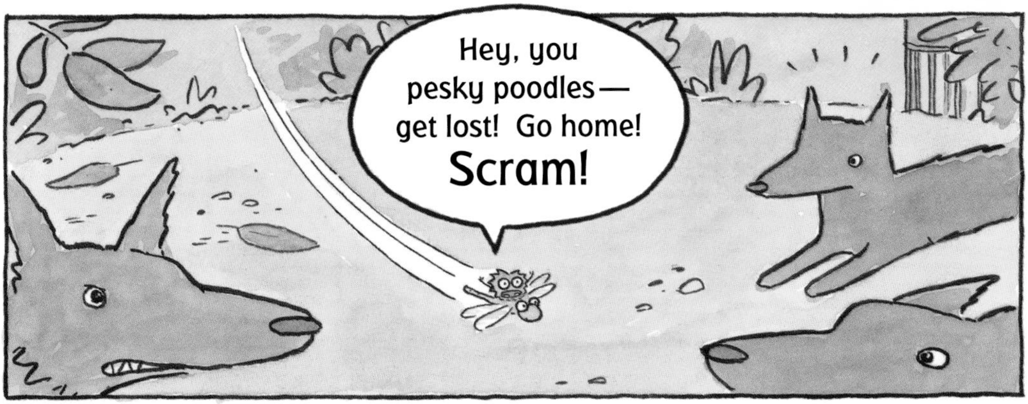
Hey, you pesky poodles — get lost! Go home! Scram!

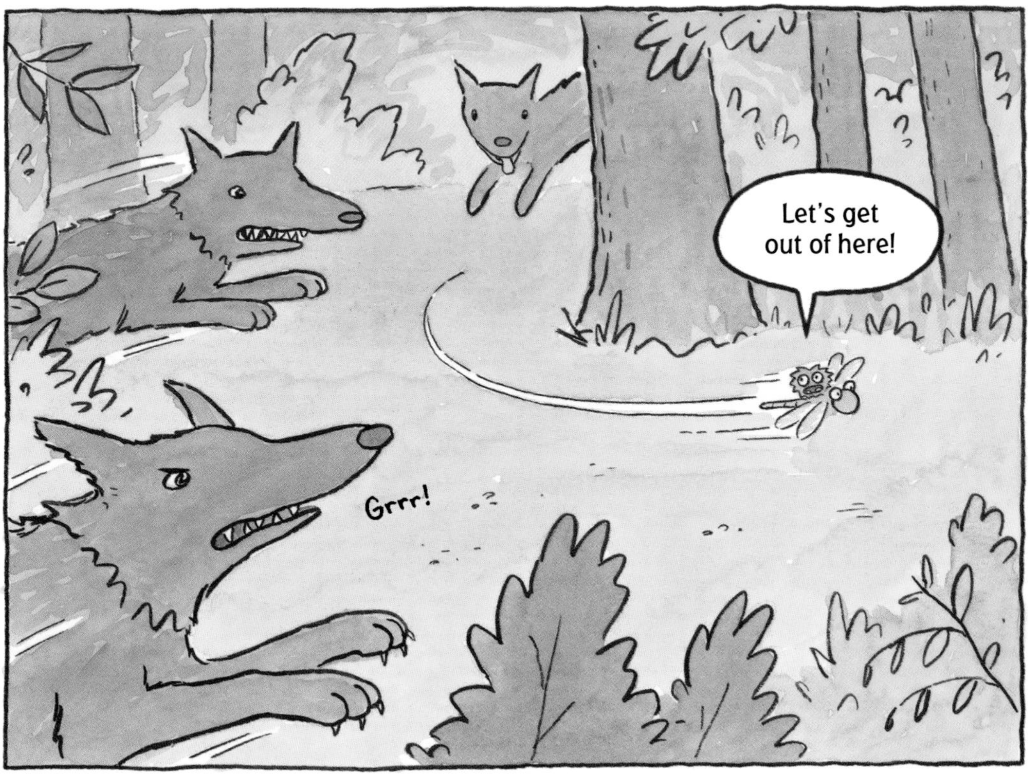
Let's get out of here!
Grrr!

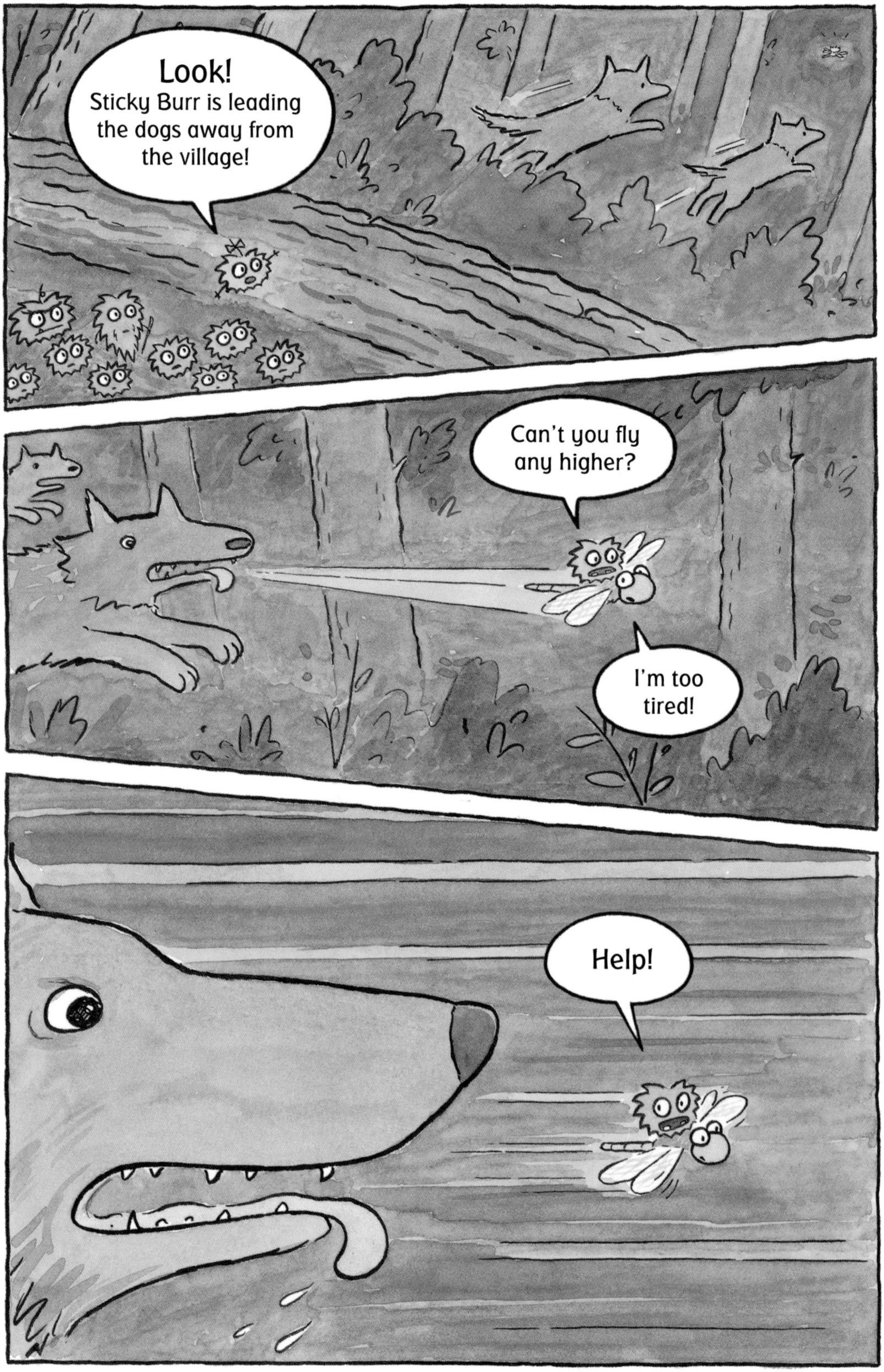
Look!
Sticky Burr is leading the dogs away from the village!
Can't you fly any higher?
I'm too tired!
Help!

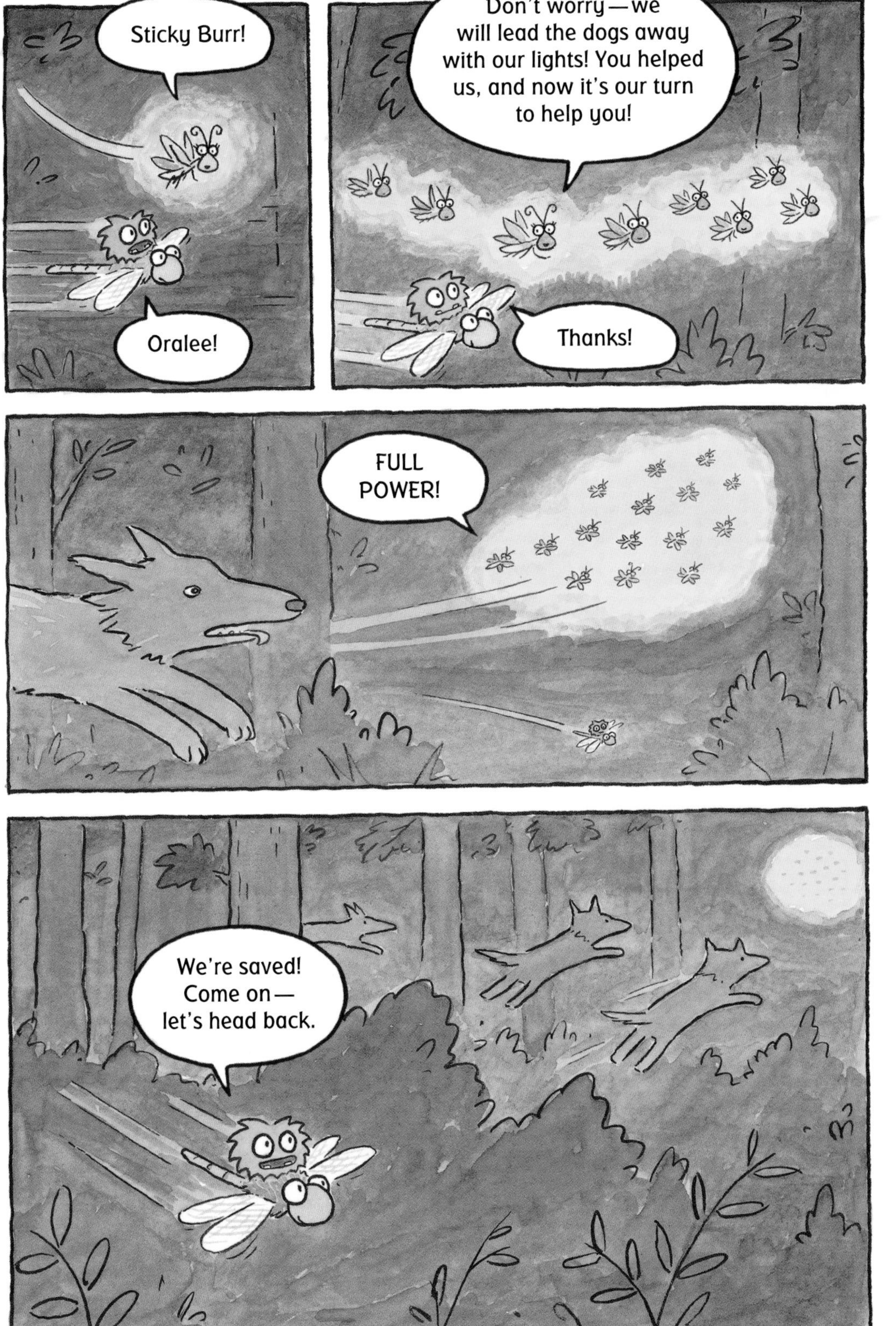
Sticky Burr!
Oralee!
Don't worry—we will lead the dogs away with our lights! You helped us, and now it's our turn to help you!
Thanks!
FULL POWER!
We're saved! Come on—let's head back.

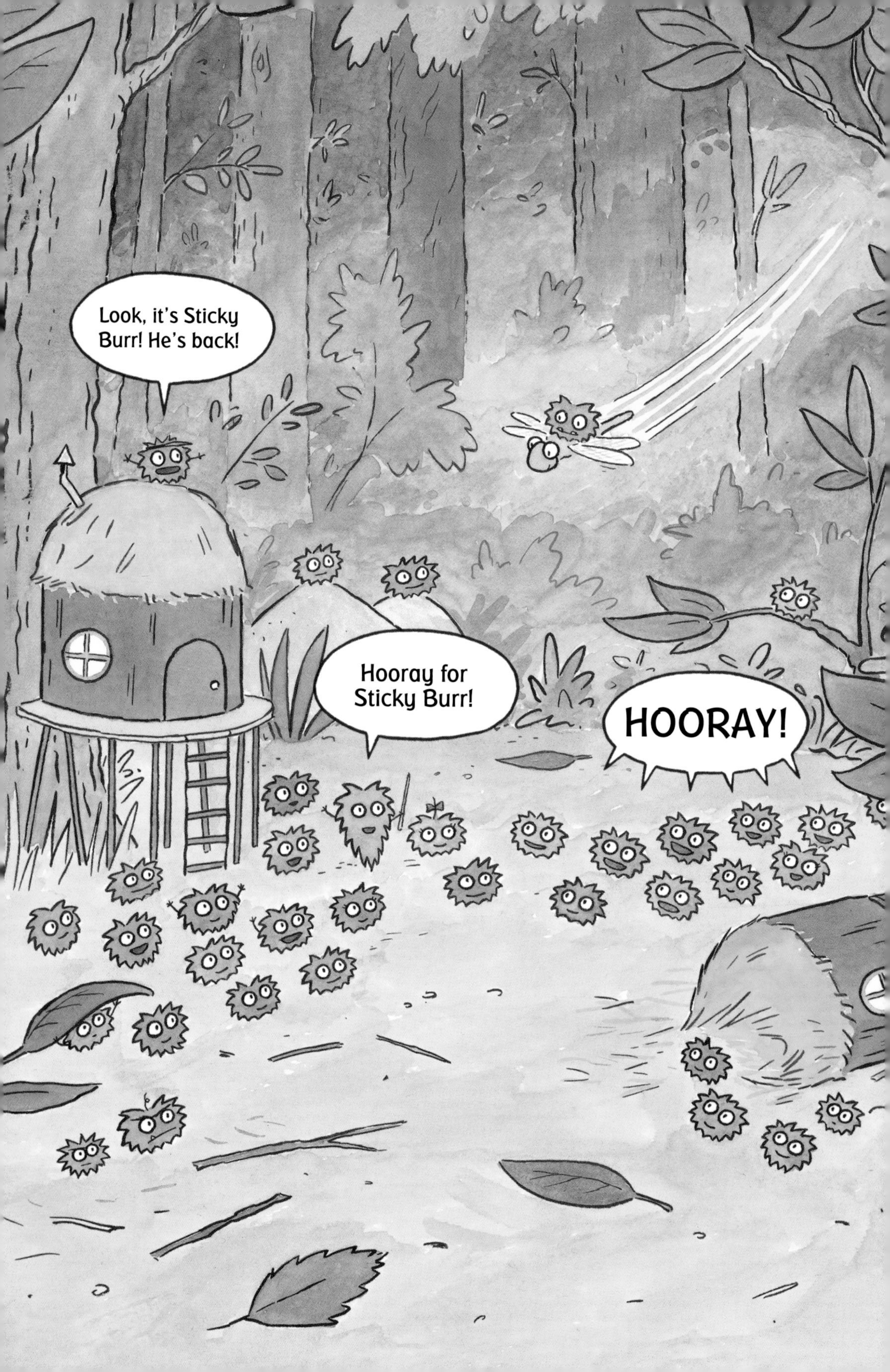
Look, it's Sticky Burr! He's back!
Hooray for Sticky Burr!
HOORAY!

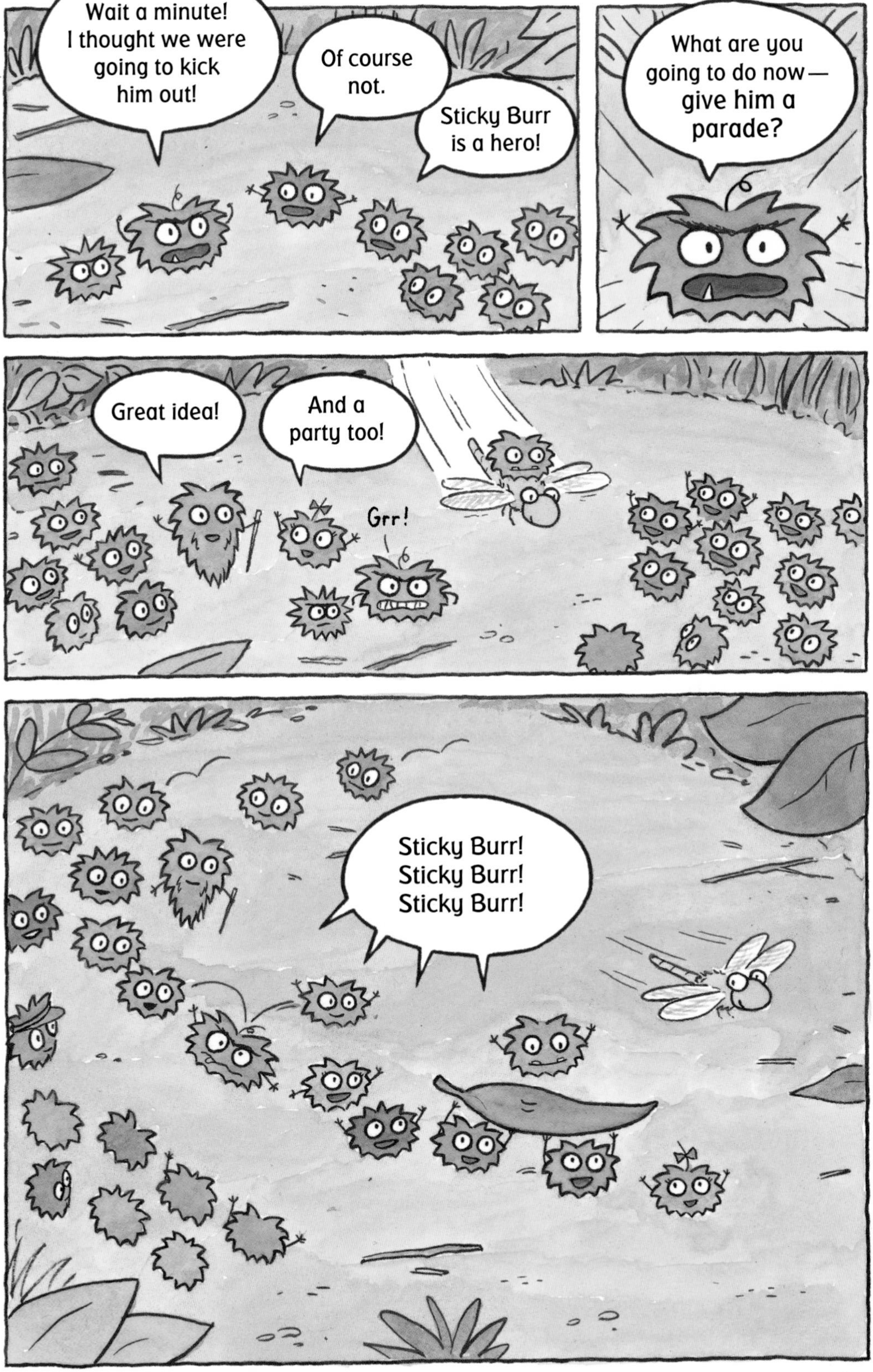
Wait a minute! I thought we were going to kick him out!
Of course not.
Sticky Burr is a hero!
What are you going to do now— give him a parade?
Great idea!
And a party too!
Grr!
Sticky Burr! Sticky Burr! Sticky Burr!

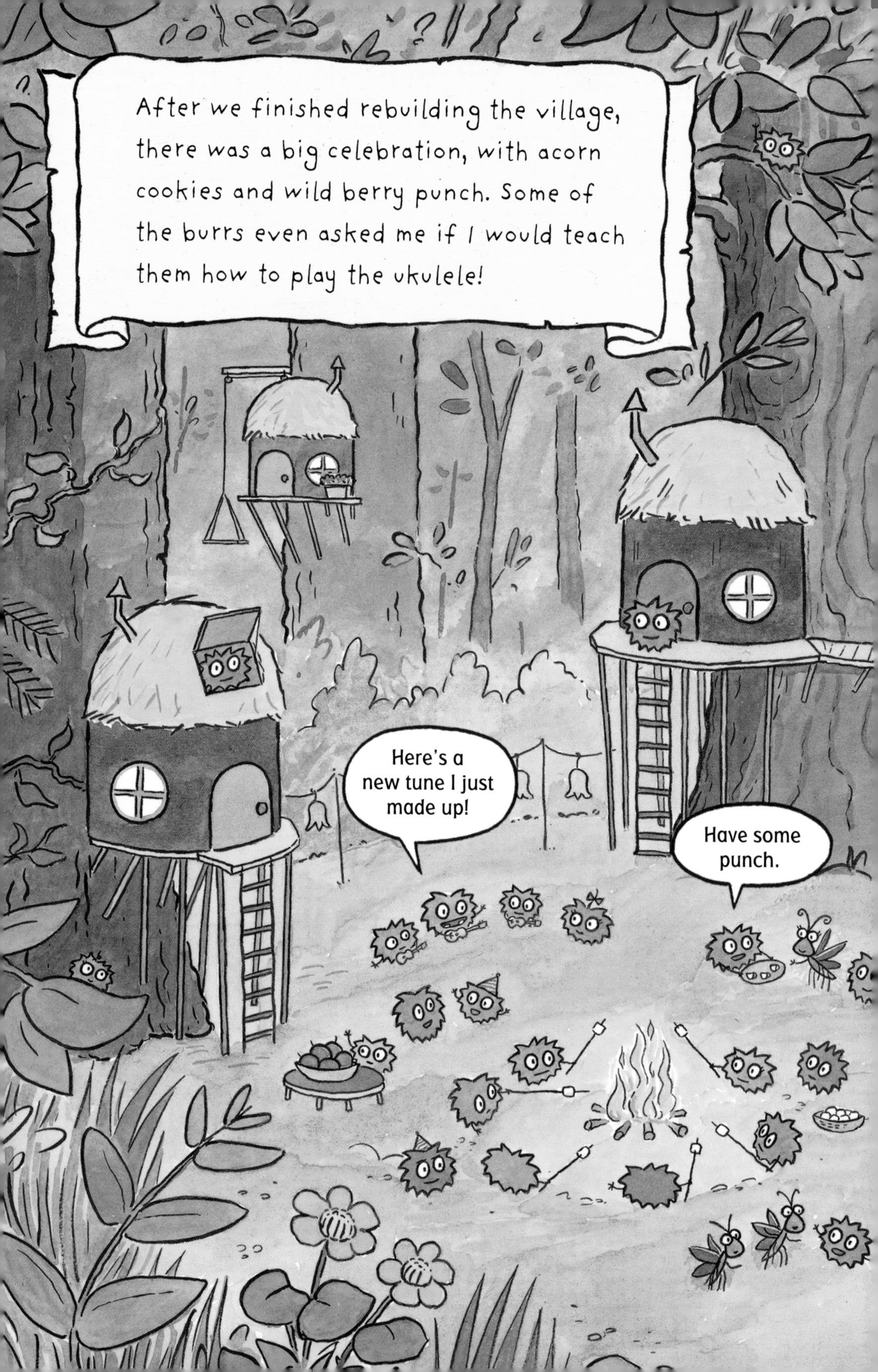
After we finished rebuilding the village, there was a big celebration, with acorn cookies and wild berry punch. Some of the burrs even asked me if I would teach them how to play the ukulele!
Here's a new tune I just made up!
Have some punch.

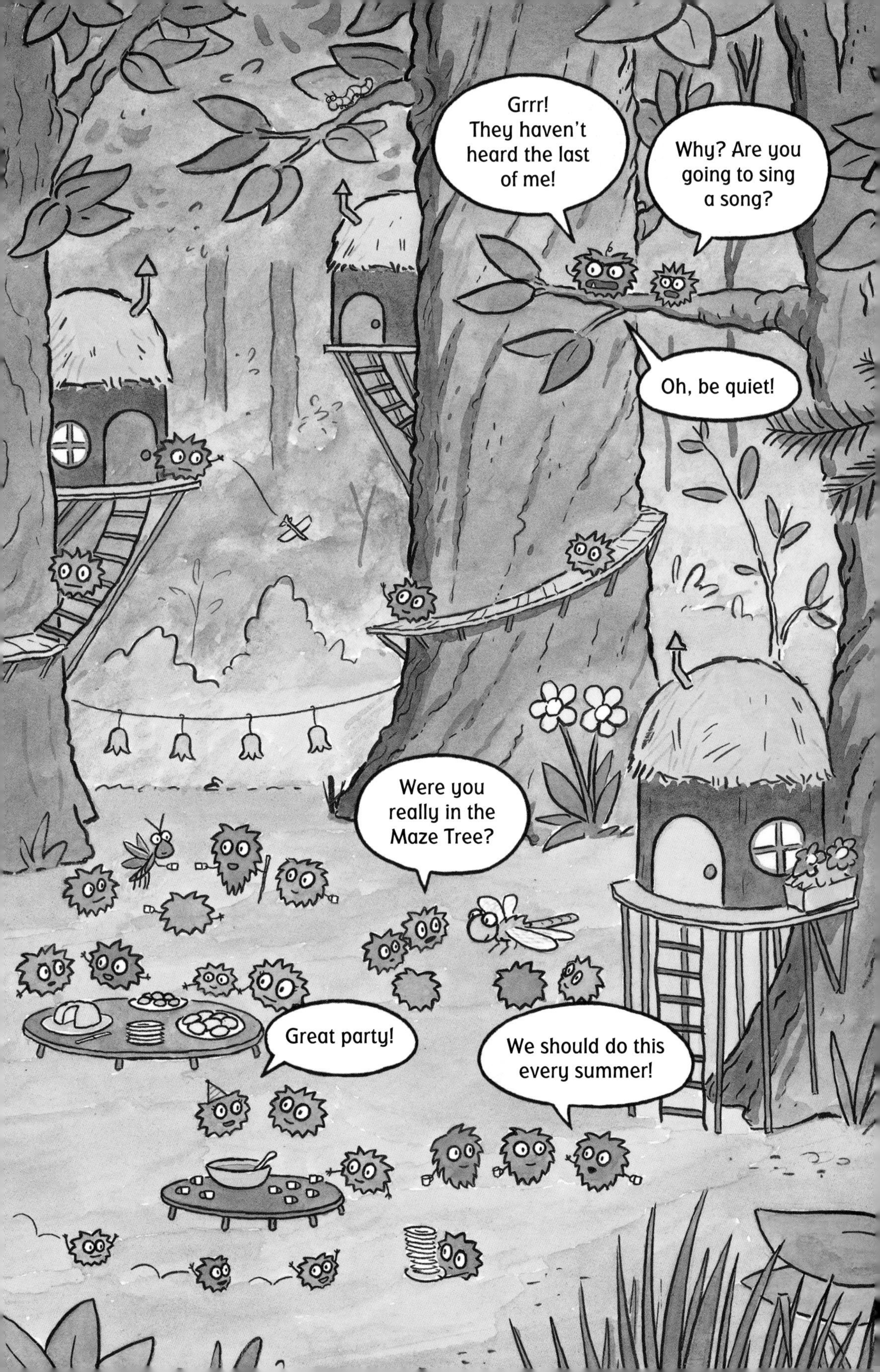

Grrr! They haven't heard the last of me!
Why? Are you going to sing a song?
Oh, be quiet!
Were you really in the Maze Tree?
Great party!
We should do this every summer!

Later, we climbed the tallest tree and looked at the stars. It was a beautiful night.

Mossy Burr says stars are like burrs, and I think she's right. Each of us tries to shine out in the darkness and be seen. And every once in a while, we are.

EPILOGUE

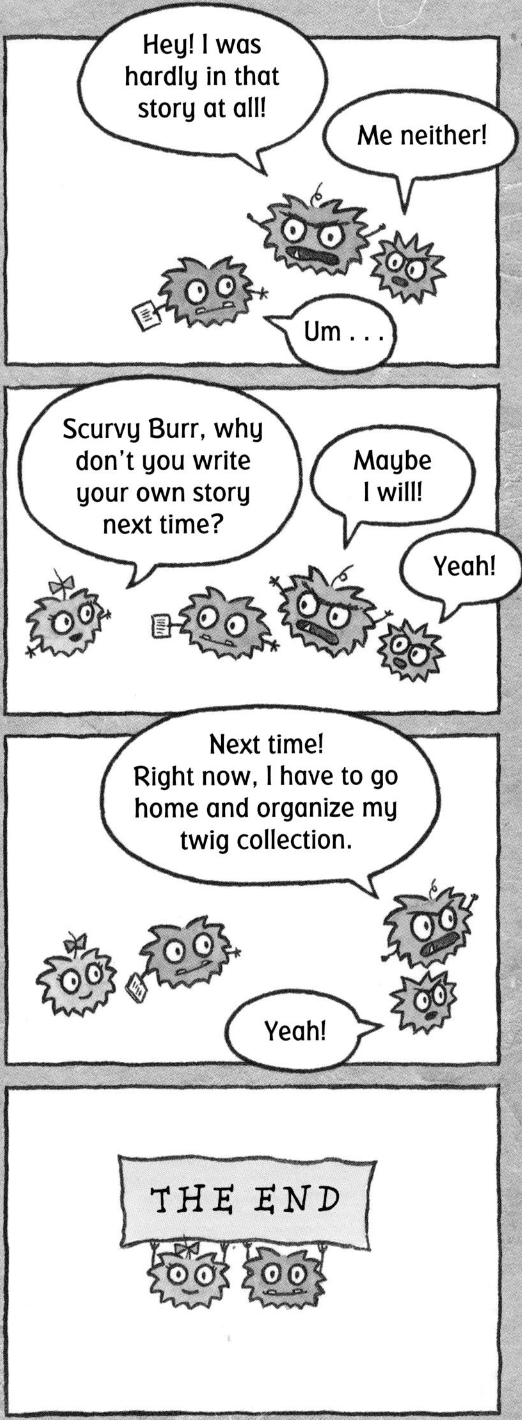
Hey! I was hardly in that story at all!
Me neither!
Um . . .
Scurvy Burr, why don't you write your own story next time?
Maybe I will!
Yeah!
Next time! Right now, I have to go home and organize my twig collection.
Yeah!
THE END

THE BURRWOOD GAZETTE

SUMMER ISSUE

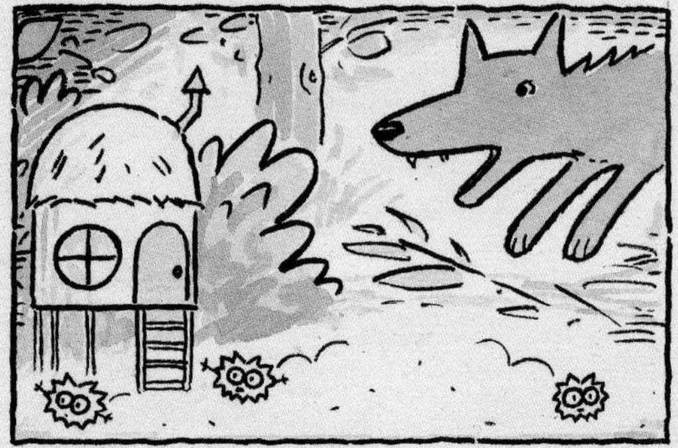

WILD DOGS WRECK VILLAGE

The Burr Village was recently destroyed by a pack of wild dogs. Luckily, Sticky Burr led the dogs away with the help of some friendly lightning bugs. The wild dogs often roam the forest during the summer and are known for their fierce appetites. However, it is not true that they eat burrs for supper. "That's just a myth," said local dog expert Fluffy Burr.

MAZE TREE DISCOVERED

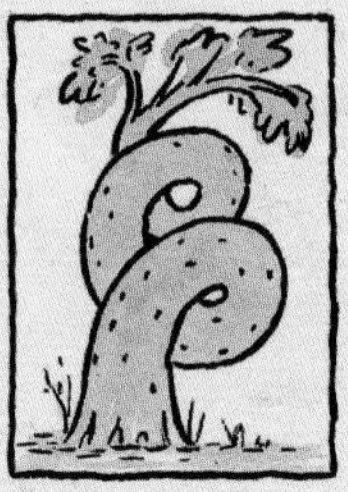

A rare tree was discovered in Dragonfly Swamp by Sticky Burr and Draffle. According to tree expert Walking Stick, the Maze Tree is filled with winding tunnels, which are quite easy to get lost in. Sticky Burr and Draffle not only escaped from the tree; they also helped rescue a group of lightning bugs who had lost their way. This autumn, the Explorers Club plans an expedition to visit the tree and study it more closely.

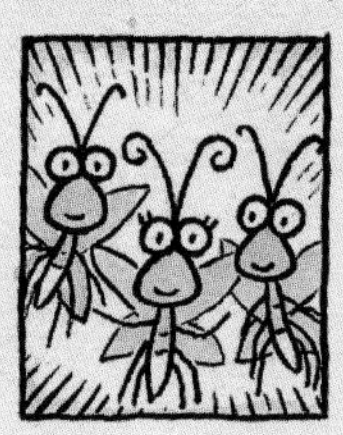

HARVEST SEASON APPROACHES

It has been a busy summer for our local gardeners. Crops of sunflowers, beans, and potatoes have been better than ever, according to Tansy Burr of the Burrwood Garden Club. "The flowers are growing like weeds!" she said. "Even the weeds are growing like weeds!" There will be a harvest fair this fall, with prizes for the best vegetables and flowers.

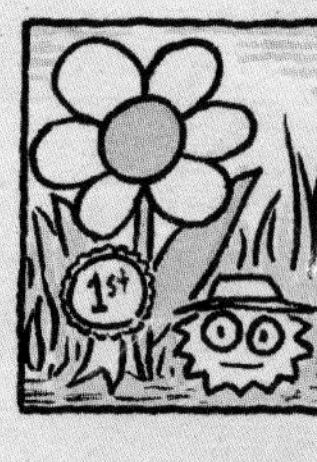
1st

ART EXHIBIT PLANNED

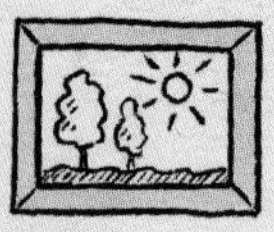

The first Burrwood art exhibit will be held this summer. All burrs are invited to submit a drawing, painting, or sculpture. "I'm making a squirrel out of pinecones!" said Balsam Burr, who lives in a pine tree. Other burrs are planning to make leaf prints, wood carvings, and bark paintings. If you are interested in participating, contact Sticky Burr.

LETTERS TO THE EDITOR

Dear Editor,

I am sick of all these cheerful and unprickly activities in our village. Please stop writing about them!

Signed, **Scurvy Burr**

Dear Editor,

Someone has been trampling the daisies in my garden. I wish that someone would stop doing it. Thank you.

Signed, **Thistle Burr**

Dear Editor,

Thank you to everyone who helped put the village back together after the wild dogs trampled it. Well done!

Signed, **Elder Burr**

NATURE NOTES by Sticky Burr

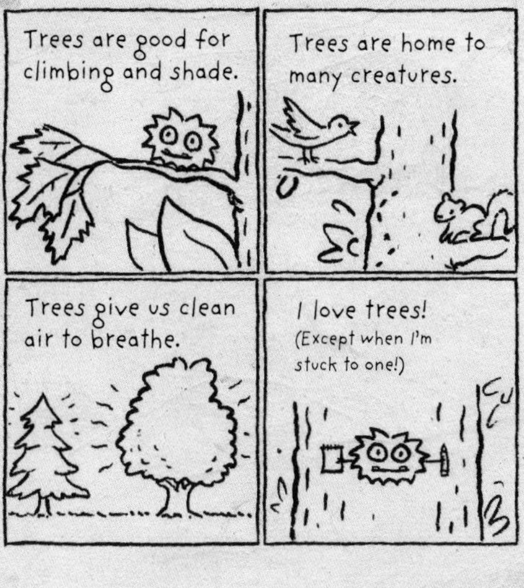

Trees are good for climbing and shade.
Trees are home to many creatures.
Trees give us clean air to breathe.
I love trees!
(Except when I'm stuck to one!)

EVENTS

SUMMER SPORTS

The annual Burrwood Summer Games will be held next week. Events will include acorn throwing, rock climbing, leaf jumping, and the oak tree marathon, in which burrs run around the big oak tree five times. Sign up at the Burrwood Town Hall.

EXPLORERS CLUB TO MEET

The Burrwood Explorers Club, led by Mossy Burr, will have its first meeting at sunrise on Midsummer's Day by the hollow log. Any burrs interested in exploring the vast and wonderful expanse of Burrwood Forest, please come and join in. (Bring a bag lunch.)

ADVERTISEMENTS

GRASSHOPPER'S SCHOOL OF KARATE AND TAI CHI

COME IN FOR A FREE LESSON ANY AFTERNOON! ALL BURRS AND INSECTS WELCOME. WE ARE LOCATED IN THE GRASSY MEADOW BY THE DUTCH ELM.

BRISTLE BURR'S ROOFING SERVICE

THATCHED ROOFS, REASONABLE RATES. SIGN-UP SHEET AT THE HOLLOW OAK.

VEGETABLES FOR SALE

FRESH CARROTS, OATS, PEAS, BEANS, AND BARLEY. GROWN LOCALLY. VISIT TANSY BURR'S FARM STAND. (LOOK FOR THE BIG SUNFLOWER!)

The Burrwood Gazette is published several times a year by Burrwood Press.
Editor in Chief: Sticky Burr Reporter: Mossy Burr Events: Nettle Burr
Bring your news articles to our office in the Sycamore tree.

Stuck on a Tree
a song by Sticky Burr

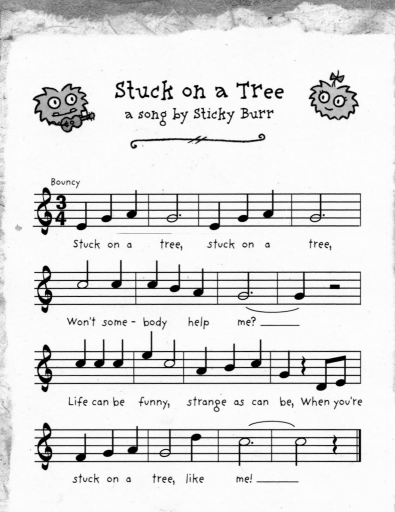

Bouncy

Stuck on a tree, stuck on a tree,

Won't some-body help me? ___

Life can be funny, strange as can be, When you're

stuck on a tree, like me! ___

(Try singing in a two-part round)